"THERE HAS NEVER BEEN ANYTHING CASUAL ABOUT THE FEELINGS WE HAVE FOR EACH OTHER ..."

Joe moved closer, his mouth poised only inches from Katherine's, and she instinctively raised her face to his. Her breath caught in her throat as they looked quietly into one another's eyes.

"There has been nothing but intense passion in the way you make me feel," Joe whispered, his mouth tracing butterfly-like kisses over hers. "It's scary, but I can't let it go now that you're back again."

Katherine's mouth parted slowly, opening itself to Joe's ardent demands. Lightly, teasingly, he touched her and it seemed as though a jolt of electricity had passed through her entire body. She clung to him as a surge of desire and need threatened to rob her of her senses ...

BREE THOMAS has lived on bases from Florida to Midway Island as the daughter of a Navy pilot. Now she is happily married and settled in Crestline, California, where, in addition to writing, she enjoys dabbling in crafts of one sort or another at all times, practicing her skills as a movie-trivia buff, and reading voraciously.

Dear Reader:

The editors of Rapture Romance have only one thing to say—thank you! At a time when there are so many books to choose from, you have welcomed ours with open arms, trying new authors, coming back again and again, and writing us of your enthusiasm. Frankly, we're thrilled!

In fact, the response has been so great that we feel confident that you are ready for more stories which explore all the possibilities that exist when today's men and women fall in love. We are proud to announce that we will now be publishing six titles each month, because you've told us that four Rapture Romances simply aren't enough. Of course, we won't substitute quantity for quality! We will continue to select only the finest of sensual love stories, stories in which the passionate physical expression of love is the glorious culmination of the entire experience of falling in love.

And please keep writing to us! We love to hear from our readers, and we take your comments and opinions seriously. If you have a few minutes, we would appreciate your filling out the questionnaire at the back of this book, or feel free to write us at the address below. Some of our readers have asked how they can write to their favorite authors, and we applaud their thoughtfulness. Writers need to hear from their fans, and while we cannot give out addresses, we are more than happy to forward any mail.

Happy reading!

Robin Grunder

Rapture Romance
1633 Broadway
New York, NY 10019

LOVE'S JOURNEY HOME

by

Bree Thomas

RAPTURE ROMANCE

NEW AMERICAN LIBRARY

TIMES MIRROR

For Martha Millard,
a lady who is everything an agent
should be, and for Clare Zion,
who brings new meaning to the word editor.
And once again, for Hal.

PUBLISHER'S NOTE

This novel is a work of fiction. Names, characters, places, and incidents either are the product of the author's imagination or are used fictitiously, and any resemblance to actual persons, living or dead, events, or locales is entirely coincidental.

NAL BOOKS ARE AVAILABLE AT QUANTITY DISCOUNTS
WHEN USED TO PROMOTE PRODUCTS OR SERVICES.
FOR INFORMATION PLEASE WRITE TO PREMIUM MARKETING DIVISION,
THE NEW AMERICAN LIBRARY, INC., 1633 BROADWAY,
NEW YORK, NEW YORK 10019.

Copyright © 1983 by Bree Thomas

SIGNET, SIGNET CLASSIC, MENTOR, PLUME, MERIDIAN AND NAL BOOKS
are published by The New American Library, Inc.,
1633 Broadway, New York, New York 10019

First Printing, December, 1983

1 2 3 4 5 6 7 8 9

PRINTED IN THE UNITED STATES OF AMERICA

Chapter One

❧

Looming dark and shadowed in the dimming twilight, the mountain was larger than she remembered. Usually a second look at once-cherished places made the memory of them feel insignificant and small. But now, as she drove along the new freeway beyond Baseline, Katherine Mallory peered up at the San Bernardino mountain range and felt strangely comforted by its intimidating expanse, as though the mountain was strong enough to make everything all right again.

Her expensive new silver Mercedes 450 SL convertible swayed slightly, protesting neglect, and Katherine quickly settled back in the seat, forcing her attention on the unfamiliar road ahead. The passing of fifteen years had left its mark, eroding the landscape at the base of the mountains. Glittering neon signs heralded the presence of gas stations and fast-food chains on almost every busy, traffic-congested surface street. Suburbia, the American dream, exploded in tract homes that littered the basin and snaked over the gently rising foothills.

For the third time in ten minutes Katherine

forced back a tremulous sigh. A sign up ahead bore the legend "Mountain Resort Communities, next right." Katherine eased off the freeway and stopped at the red light. The clicking of the turn indicator echoed rhythmically in the silence of the car.

Less than an hour to go, Katherine thought excitedly. She turned on the headlights just as the signal turned green and, veering to the right, she started the last two-mile stretch before the highway narrowed into the single lane that would sashay up the side of the mountain. Her hand shook uncontrollably as she replaced it on the steering wheel. Less than an hour to go.

Even thinking about Rimforest, the small community where she had been born and raised, made Katherine's eyes begin to fill with tears. Lately, it didn't take much to make her cry. A sentimental song, a sad movie, a broken fingernail; all were guaranteed to reduce Katherine to a quivering mass of depression.

Snap out of it, girl, Katherine reprimanded herself sternly. Get a hold on yourself!

As she had numerous times over the years, Katherine asked herself: What would Leanne do? How would Leanne handle this?

Leanne Cameron, Katherine Mallory's alter ego. Leanne Davis Addiston Tremayne Cameron, the much-married superbitch, the schemer everyone loved to hate, the temperamental thread that wove itself through the lives of everyone who populated Bells Ferry, the mythical locale of the network's most successful "continuing daytime drama," *Bright Promise*. From troublesome teenager to neurotic adult, Katherine had played the part of Leanne Cameron to perfection. In fact, she was so convincing that even she was beginning to wonder where Leanne left off and Katherine began.

Don't think about it, Katherine scolded again. You have two glorious weeks to yourself. Don't worry about it now.

Katherine's contract was being renegotiated by the network and her agent, Larry Michaels. While they were coming to terms, her character was being written out of the show. Leanne was having a grand time of it in New York, spending part of the enormous sum she had just collected after divorcing husband number three.

As for Leanne's creator—well, Katherine had rented a cabin and was planning to kick back and relax for a week before attending her high school class's fifteenth reunion. Another week's respite was to follow the reunion. It was the first real, get-off-by-herself vacation Katherine had been able to plan in years.

If Mother was still alive, Katherine thought with a wry smile, this is the last place on earth she would want me to visit. London, Katmandu, New Orleans, Pittsburgh. Anyplace but Rimforest!

Small towns breed nothing but small-time dreams, Katherine's mother had always said. Did I scrimp and save to pay for dancing and drama lessons so you could go running back to Rimforest when things got a little tough? Did we go so far, so fast, for you to end up in a town with a lumberyard mentality?

Elizebeth Mallory was determined that Katherine not spend her life in a wood-frame two-bedroom house set off from the highway on a dirt road. *Her* daughter would have more than weather-toughened skin and living week-to-week on a small paycheck that never seemed to stretch past Thursday. When Katherine's father had died, Elizabeth Mallory's single-minded ambitions had only intensified.

Years of dance and voice class, catalog modeling assignments, and occasional television commercials had finally ended with all the pieces falling into just the right places. In a world where physical beauty was an aspiring actress's greatest asset, Katherine had the right look for the right show at the right time. *Bright Promise* needed an ingenue to play young Leanne Davis, the spoiled fourteen-year-old niece of the show's most prominent family. Katherine's pale, cool beauty caught the producer's eye. She had what they termed the "moneyed" look. She was tall and willowy, delicately boned and graceful. Baby-fine, naturally blond hair framed a heart-shaped face dominated by large, heavily lashed dark brown eyes. Smooth, full lips added a touch of petulance and scorn and a promise of sensuality. A lightly freckled aristocratic nose gave mischievous relief to Katherine's almost overpowering beauty.

The open auditions, the callbacks, lunch with the show's production staff—it all happened so quickly, Katherine was breathless. She allowed herself to be swept along, dazed by her sudden importance and the first taste of power her loveliness would command.

And despite a limited education and even less experience in the world, Elizebeth Mallory used her own instinctive gifts for manipulation and foresight to parlay a three-month contract with option into a career that had, so far, spanned fifteen years.

Just look at your girl now, Mama, Katherine mused sadly. I'm everything you ever wanted me to be, a product of our ambitions. Still, my hand has a tremor I can't quite control, and I spend most of my time trying not to cry. I bite my lips to keep them from quivering and I'm filled with anxiety and I don't know why. Other than that, everything's fine.

Don't think about it, the tiny warning voice in the back of Katherine's mind commanded. Later. Later, when you're rested and feeling stronger. You can handle anything when you're feeling up to it.

It's taken you fifteen years to make the three-hour drive from Los Angeles to Rimforest. Enjoy it. Revel in it. The air smells like green, living things, and a blanket of stars is draped over the mountain. Enjoy it! You're going home.

The road widened every few miles to permit a passing lane for faster, lighter cars to move past the slower traffic. Katherine felt like she was involved in a zany game of bumper tag. She was crazy, making this drive on a Friday night. She should have remembered that the snow conditions farther up at Big Bear Lake beckoned every ski bum and snow bunny within two hundred miles. Luckily the Rimforest area wasn't covered yet so there was no need to attach the tire chains in the trunk.

Beyond Crestline and Valley of Enchantment, past Lake Gregory and Twin Peaks, Katherine moved with the agonizingly slow traffic along Rim of the World Highway. She thought wistfully how beautiful the scenic drive was during the day. Now the silver beams of car headlights cut through the misty air and sent long, shimmering lines criss-crossing through the towering trees and thick foliage just beyond the road.

Katherine smiled happily, flushed with pleasure. It was all beginning to come back to her now. Here, just off the road, was the house where Mr. Cluny lived. He carved lovely little animals with his whittling knife, so tiny they could fit in the closed palm of a hand. There, coming up just around the corner, was the cabin whose owners had habitually forgotten to lock the back door when they departed after a weekend visit. That open door had proved too tempting to the more adventurous local kids in Katherine's day. Many a party had been held in that pretty little cabin while the Benedicts slept peacefully unaware in their permanent Orange County home down below.

Katherine laughed softly and tossed her head, remembering how she had always been too frightened to participate in the first few impromptu parties. And, of course, the one night she chose to go along was the same night the county sheriff cruised in from the Twin Peaks substation and—

Just up ahead, on the left, was her turnoff.

The dimly lit wooden sign read "Flynn's Forest Retreat." Katherine slowed and made the turn onto a dark, twisting street. The surface of the street was falling away at the sides and pitted with gaping holes large enough to hold basketballs. She grimaced, thinking of what her mechanic would have to say about the Mercedes' alignment when she got back from this little jaunt. Already the high altitude was playing hell with the car's timing. She should have had it reset before coming up the mountain. The repairs for the precise, temperamental Mercedes were going to cost a small fortune, not to mention the indignant disbelief on the mechanic's face when he found out how she had mistreated the expensive sports car.

As soon as the thought flitted into her mind, Katherine tossed it aside impatiently. What did she care how much it cost or what someone she hardly knew had to say? *That* was a Leanne Cameron thought. Only Leanne would concentrate on the trivial and let it overpower her enjoyment of the moment.

I must be going crazy, Katherine thought with a slight frown. Leanne is beginning to creep into every aspect of my life, even the passenger seat of this car!

It had been far too long since Katherine had been able to take off the Leanne character like a coat and leave it behind at the studio. Every year Leanne got more demanding, more ruthless. And every year Katherine Mallory seemed to find herself responding to the world outside *Bright Promise* with a little less spontaneity and joy.

Not this time! Katherine's delicate jaw clenched

with determination. I'm going to have a marvelous, carefree time even if I have to take Leanne into the forest and murder her.

The jolt of the Mercedes lurching out of another chuckhole accentuated Katherine's resolve. Maneuvering along the last series of turns in the road, Katherine slowed the car and came to a stop in front of the Retreat.

Nestled among the towering pines that almost blotted out the starry sky, the two-story chalet beckoned to her. Golden light flickered behind delicately scalloped red shutters. Smoke drifted from a chimney of perfectly matched native stone. A single spotlight cast its glow on the narrow dirt road that ran along the side of the chalet and led to the half-dozen tiny cabins behind the main residence.

Katherine turned off the engine and reached back into the well behind the seats, retrieving a corduroy blazer. She slipped into the jacket and got out of the car. Cold, biting air assaulted her immediately, slipping down inside the low, buttoned front of her silk blouse and rushing up the folds of her soft suede skirt. Gravel and leaves crackled beneath her boots as she made her way to the screened front door of the office. She hesitated at the door a moment, unsure whether she should knock discreetly or simply walk in unannounced. Choosing the polite tact, Katherine knocked softly and waited.

"Come in out of that weather!" A series of deep, rattling coughs erupted from within the office. "Come on in."

Nodding silently, Katherine passed through the

door. Her attention was immediately caught by the Ben Franklin stove in the corner that was heating the room. It was difficult to tear her eyes away from the warmth that shimmered above the cast iron.

"Mrs. Flynn?" Katherine began to dig around in her purse for the postcard she had recently received. "I'm Katherine Mallory. I have the confirmation on a cabin somewhere here in all this mess."

"No need, child," Mrs. Flynn told Katherine as she took up her position behind the desk. "Everything's ready for you, Miss Mallory. Just—" Mrs. Flynn sneezed suddenly, puncuating the sound with another long series of racking coughs. "Sign in and I'll—" She sneezed again and shook her head in exasperation.

For the first time, Katherine took a good look at Mrs. Flynn. Bundled in a heavy sweater, with woolen muffler wrapped around her neck, the tiny woman appeared to be waging a losing battle against pneumonia. She looked terrible. Her nose was pink and chapped from blowing. A tissue dangled listlessly in her hand, ready to ward off the next attack. Behind round granny glasses, Mrs. Flynn's red-rimmed eyes teared and watered helplessly. The deeply wrinkled lines of her face were flushed with fever.

"You should be in bed." Katherine felt a little foolish suggesting something so obvious, but it was all she could think of to say.

"Should be a lot of things." Mrs. Flynn's short laugh was broken by a fit of coughing. "Rich, beautiful, young again. Healthy wouldn't be too hard to take, either, but 'should be' doesn't run the Retreat."

"Don't bother with me, Mrs. Flynn." Katherine took the pen and scribbled her name in the register, smiling sympathetically. "Just point me in the right direction. I can find the cabin on my own. I really feel quite guilty about keeping you up so late."

"Heavens, no! The office says open—sick or well, sun or snow—until nine o'clock every night of the week. Besides, I'm waiting for a visit from the doctor. I can't get in to the village with this damn-fool cold, so he comes out here after office hours."

"Oh, that's nice." Katherine sighed, remembering the times Doc Taley had called upon her mother's house. He had been old even when Katherine was a child; he must be ancient now.

Katherine was just thinking how nice it would be to wait around and see Doc Taley when the screen door opened and shut behind her. She looked across the desk to see Mrs. Flynn's face light up with relief and pleasure.

"Well, Doctor," Mrs. Flynn said as she frowned teasingly, "I'd just about given up hope of seeing you tonight."

"Busy day, Moll. And . . ." The doctor's voice trailed off as he caught sight of Molly Flynn's latest guest and absentmindedly set his medical bag on a table by the door.

Katherine turned slowly toward the sound of the voice—that deep, masculine, and familiar voice—and the oddest, most disorienting thought flew into her mind.

Dum-da-dum-dum! The music swells and the camera zooms in on my stricken, disbelieving face. Then a slow fade and I have two minutes of commercial time to regain my composure and set up for the next scene.

But no, this wasn't magic time, this was real life, and the same woman who had won two daytime Emmys for her professionalism, the same woman who had memorized thousands of pages of witty dialogue and breezed through a hundred confrontations just like this, felt her mouth drop open and every syllable of the English launguage vanish from memory. All that was left was a single vocal impulse: "Joe." Katherine's brown eyes widened with recognition. "Joe!"

"I wish you weren't so surprised." Joe Mercer pretended to flinch. "It's embarrassing. How ya' doing?" He crossed the room in a blur of sudden movement, and before Katherine had a chance to react, he drew her into a quick embrace and planted a kiss on her cheek, whispering, "You're looking good, Katherine. It's been a long time."

Yesterday, Katherine thought inanely. It's been fifteen years but it feels like yesterday. And I'm standing here with my jaw on the floor, acting like a tongue-tied kid.

"You look wonderful too, Joe." It was standard stuff but she was still a bit dazed. And besides, it was true.

He stepped back to look at her for a moment, but his hands remained on her shoulders. Then he shrugged lightly. "Well, I'd better get to work. Maybe we can get together sometime before the reunion. You know, talk about old times. Swap lies." As though he just then realized he was still holding on to her, Joe's hands dropped suddenly to his sides. "I'll give you a call, okay?"

"I'd like that." Katherine smiled hesitantly, surprised again by the hurried pace of her heartbeat and the strangled sensation in her throat. She swallowed hard and watched as Joe picked up his medical bag, then took Molly Flynn's arm and led her gently to an overstuffed chair near the Franklin stove.

She supposed the polite thing to do was inquire after her key and leave the two of them alone, but at that moment, nothing short of dynamite could have shaken her loose. Instead, she leaned up against the desk, fascinated by the metamorphosis that changed Joe from ordinary man to doctor of medicine. Katherine had always been slightly in awe of doctors. The complicated, somehow secret medical jargon. The feeling that they knew something they weren't telling. The sure conviction that a doctor had it in his power to make everything all right again.

"Well, Molly, looks like you've got another case," Joe said as he bent to examine her. Katherine knew her presence was all but forgotten. "I could set my calendar by you. If Molly Flynn has her first bout with bronchial infection, it must be January. How long did you wait to call me this time?"

Joe pulled out a stethoscope and draped it around his neck. He slipped a thermometer under Molly's tongue, catching her in mid-sentence while she was promising, wide-eyed and innocent, that she had phoned in at the very first sign of illness.

"You have to take better care of yourself," Joe scolded quietly. "Putting off calling me won't make the cold go away, you know. It only takes me longer to get you well." Having issued what appeared to be a standard reprimand between them, Joe stood up and rubbed his hands together. "Now, how about a cup of that famous coffee you always have on the brew?"

Molly grunted, balancing the thermometer between her lips, and pointed to the sideboard near the desk, where Joe could help himself. When he turned around, he seemed suprised to find Katherine still in the office.

"My key?" She flushed at being caught so obviously interested. "I still don't have my key."

Molly lifted the thermometer briefly. "Well, no need to rush off. Doctor Joe hasn't gotten to the nasty part yet. Have a cup of coffee with him while I—" A scathing look from Joe was all the prompting Molly needed to clamp shut her mouth and settle back in her chair quietly.

Joe was standing beside Katherine now and he picked up an empty cup to offer her coffee. It took a second to get past the feeling that Joe's expression had gone from friendly welcome to cautious scrutiny, but Katherine nodded mutely. The coffee smelled good and the steam was rising out of the pot as Joe tipped it over the cup. Katherine's cold hands slipped around the mug gratefully and raised it to her lips. She was glad to have something to divert her attention as Joe balanced on the edge of the desk only inches away from her.

Why was she having such a hard time talking to him? She was in the business of words and snappy repartee. Yet, absurd as it was, she could think of nothing to say. Really, though, she shouldn't have been all that surprised. Joe had always had that effect on her. "Intimidating" was the word she was searching for.

"You've caused quite a stir with this reunion thing," Joe said, breaking the uncomfortable silence. "The organizing committee started sending up flares the moment you wired you were coming." Something very close to a smirk crossed his lips and then was replaced by a casual expression. "Why'd you come up so early?"

"I needed some breathing space, I guess." Katherine shrugged gracefully. "And I wanted some time to look around. You know, see what's changed, what's stayed the same. You, Joe," she said, raising a brow archly and feeling more in control, "are a real surprise."

"You aren't," he countered quickly. "Except maybe you're even prettier now than when you left. Must be all that rarefied air in L.A."

"Thank you." Katherine's response was automatic and more than a little bewildered. Somehow the flattering words didn't feel much like a compliment. The initial excitement she had experienced at coming upon Joe in this unlikely manner was quickly wearing thin.

She fell silent again and lifted the cup to her mouth, stealing a glance at Joe as he gazed straight ahead. As far as looks went, he was no slouch himself. Never had been. A few inches over six feet tall, Joe had wide, thickly muscled shoulders that tapered to a slim, firm waist. Not an ounce of fat on him, Katherine thought a little reproachfully, and I'll bet he never has to watch the amount of sweets and starches he eats. Probably just one of those people who are blessed with a system that burns off the calories quicker than they're consumed.

And that tan! How does he keep that tan? The dead of winter and Joe looks like he's been lolling around the beaches of Bermuda. Even his light brown hair, brushed carelessly over his ears in thick waves, was sun-streaked. Bronze-toned skin made Joe's blue eyes look even bluer, or maybe it was just the soft light in the room that made him look so good. He certainly didn't look like any doctor Katherine had ever seen before, at least not outside a casting call for *Bright Promise.* Lounging against the desk, bursting with robust good health, dressed in faded jeans and a blue-and-green wool shirt, Joe looked more like a lumberjack than a doctor.

"I still can't believe this." Katherine's pale hair swayed softly as she shook her head. "You, Joe Mercer, the village sawbones."

Joe laughed shortly. "We all grow up to be something." If he was offended by Katherine's comment, he didn't show it.

"True," she agreed lamely. "But who would have guessed Joe Mercer, the rowdiest boy in Rimforest, would choose a career in medicine?"

"Right." Joe's face colored slightly. "That I chose to do something honorable with my life

came as a big shock to everyone who knows me."
Now he shifted his position so that he was facing
her. "The same could be said of you. Who would
have thought shy little Katie Mallory would grow
up to be famous for her dirty tricks and bed-
hopping?"

"Why, Joe, I'm surprised at you." Katherine
smiled as sweetly and as sarcastically as she could
manage. "A grown man mistaking reality for
fantasy. Leanne Cameron is a character I play,
not a role I live." The assumption that her own
morals paralleled those of Leanne Cameron was
wildly irritating. But worse was hearing Joe again
call her Katie, a nickname Katherine had always
hated and hadn't allowed anyone to use in years.
K-K-K-Katie. Even now she almost cringed. K-K-
K-Katie, c-c-c-come on out. Whispered in the hall-
ways at school, called out from the darkness of
the woods beyond her house, that teasing, sing-
song chant—

All right! Whatever was eating at him was his
problem, not hers. *She* was genuinely happy to
see him again, even a bit . . . Well, that wasn't
important now. But after those first few moments
of greeting, Joe was proving himself as rude and
arrogant now as when he was a boy. The only
way Katherine was ever going to enjoy this vacation and the reunion was to avoid seeing him
again.

She was poised to turn on her heel and walk
away when the sound of a muffled cough broke
through the suffocating silence in the room.

"Don't let me stop you." Molly Flynn grinned

wickedly. "I've got a feeling you're just getting to the good part."

Joe was the first to turn away. He went back over to Molly and muttered, "Show's over for tonight, Moll. Let's go into the house." He gathered up his medical bag. "I want to listen to your chest."

Molly beamed, winking broadly at Katherine, her eyes twinkling behind the granny glasses. "The man's an absolute animal. He can't wait to get the shirt off my back." She allowed Joe to guide her through the door that connected the office to her home, calling back over her shoulder, "Welcome to the Retreat, Katie. Your key is hanging on the peg marked number ten. Just like you requested, it's the most secluded . . ." The rest of what she said was lost as both she and Joe disappeared into the house.

Katherine snatched up the key, almost ripping the peg off the wall in her haste, and marched stiffly out to her car. Parked next to it was a truck that hadn't been there when she pulled into the parking area.

That figured! Didn't the big strong he-man type always drive a truck? Katherine's dark soulful eyes beseeched the starry heavens. Damn! She hadn't thought of Joe Mercer in years, but now he was like an itch under her skin and she had to scratch it. Memories came flooding back like an onrushing tidal wave, out of control.

Joey Mercer. In elementary school he had been a mop of tangled golden hair, all skinned elbows and torn pants legs, perpetual motion, taunting and teasing, running and shoving. Katherine had been the perfect foil for Joey's reign of terror. A quiet, serious little girl, she had been easily victimized, believing anything that was told her, led willingly down the primrose path.

Junior high school. The hated name-calling, whispers, snickering. Joe and his obnoxious, rowdy gang of cohorts following close on Katherine's heels, giggling and pointing, spying. That awful day the whole class went swimming and Joey unsnapped Katherine's bathing-suit top and swung it over his head like a banner, reducing Katherine to hot, embarrassed tears before relenting and returning the loathsome piece of cloth.

And in high school, the long silences and veiled, secretive looks. Joey's hell-raising took on other aspects. He became obsessed with and famous for the single-minded pursuit and conquest of every available female on the mountain.

Every girl but me, Katherine remembered with a heavy sigh. Joe all but ignored the one girl who had been the chief object of his boyhood tricks and torment. God, how that slight had made her feel ugly and inadequate.

Now, while her mind drifted backward in time, Katherine struggled to calm herself and bring into focus the gray and forgotten areas of memory. Moments, faded now and difficult to clarify, when Joe had touched her heart. Times when . . .

That night at the Benedicts' cabin. Katherine had always refused to join the others when they staged their parties, but for some reason on that night she had decided to go along with them. It was a mild summer night and, as usual, the back door to the cabin had been left unlocked. By the time Joe and his friends arrived, the living room was rocking with the sounds of music and ice chests of beer were stacked in the kitchen. Just exactly how it happened, Katherine could not now remember even under fear of torture, but she had ended up with Joe later that evening in one of the back bedrooms. And he was the sweetest, the most gentle she had ever known him to be. And it felt so good, so right. There was a sense of wonder in his kisses and the tender touch of his hands over the thin cotton blouse she wore. Only the shrill wail of the sheriff's siren as he pulled up to the cabin to answer a disturbance call prevented Katherine's name from being added to the list of Joe's triumphs.

She thought of it that way now, but at the time, he had made her feel very special. Graduation was only a few weeks away and it was she, Katherine Mallory, that he chose to ask to the prom. She was wild to go with him, to be with him, and thoughts of the upcoming dance filled nearly every minute of the day and night. But on the morning of the prom, the call had come in from *Bright Promise* and the choice for Leanne was between Katherine and one other aspiring actress, and as her mother had said, the dance was only one night out of her life.

Katherine had tried desperately to get in touch with Joe during those morning hours, but once she and her mother were at the studio it was impossible to call. The dance came and went and by the time they returned home, Joe had left the mountain for a summer of hitchhiking across the country with a friend. Katherine and her mother left Rimforest a week later and moved to a small house in West Hollywood. She never saw or heard anything about Joe Mercer again. Or anyone else in Rimforest, for that matter. Katherine's childhood was spent preparing for the future, not developing close friendships that would stand the passage of time and distance. Oh, there were a few hastily written letters between her and a girl she'd known since kindergarten, but even those dwindled away after the first year.

Face it, baby, Katherine told herself as she dumped the first of her luggage on the porch of the cabin, you've got no one to blame but yourself. You cut yourself off or at least stood by and let it happen without so much as a whimper. There's nothing here for you because when you went away, you didn't leave even a shred of yourself behind to keep the home fires burning.

Katherine was exhausted from the busy day, the long drive, the meeting with Joe, everything. Her mind was clouded and her eyes so heavy she could barely keep her thoughts from drifting.

I'll figure out what I'm going to do—stay or just go back where I belong—tomorrow, when I'm not so damned tired and upset.

Chapter Two

ॐ

The next morning, Katherine awoke stiff and sore from having spent the night, fully clothed, curled uncomfortably in a chair in front of the fireplace. The thin mountain air had done her in, creeping up on her before she had a chance to unpack and slip into bed. A roaring, crackling fire had seemed like such a good idea at the time. Even the kindling had been prepared in advance of her arrival. The last thing she remembered was setting a match to it and settling back in the chair, rubbing her hands together to get the blood circulating again.

Katherine tossed off the knit lap blanket tangled in her legs and stood up to stretch out the aches in her bones. She had a busy morning to face. The fire had long since burned out and needed tending. Clothes that were still folded in her luggage had to be hung and steamed. Underclothes and makeup should be put away in drawers. She needed a shower and her nails could use a fresh coat of polish. The curling iron had to be plugged in, and—

Whoa, girl! Katherine raised her hands in mock terror. With a schedule like that, you could have stayed home. You're on vacation, remember? Let's simplify things a bit.

Katherine's eyes swept over the room, surveying the small one-room cabin. A bathroom and compact kitchen occupied the far wall. The living area, paneled floor to ceiling with varnished pecky cedar planks, was about the size of the guest room in Katherine's Hollywood apartment. Still, the clutter had an offbeat kind of charm.

A double bed was tucked into one corner, covered by a patchwork quilt and piled high with goose-feather pillows. A slightly frayed braided oval rug covered a large portion of the hardwood floor. The tall oak wardrobe in the corner was at least seventy years old and polished to a high, mirrorlike sheen. Clusters of orange and gold leaves decorated the chintz-covered armchair that was more quaint than comfortable. Matching curtains hung from small, square-paned windows.

The sun had yet to crest the forest outside, so the cabin was dark. Katherine pushed aside the curtains and judged, from the amount of light filtering through the trees, that the hour was earlier than she would have liked. A quick glance at her watch confirmed the guess. Eight o'clock in the morning. What an unholy time to wake up on the first morning of her vacation.

Katherine laughed gaily, not really caring. She danced across the room, scooped up her makeup bag, and went into the bathroom to shower. Twenty minutes later she emerged with a scrubbed face, just a hint of color on her cheeks, and her hair wrapped in a knotted towel.

Crossing to the fireplace, she pushed back the

ash with a poker before lighting a new fire. Then she brushed and dried her hair by the heat of the flame. The luxury of taking the time to pamper herself so lazily felt terrific.

When she stood up again, Katherine dumped her makeup bag out on the bed. She sifted through its contents, removing only a wand of mascara, a bottle of moisturizer, and a specially blended brush-on kit of blusher. Everything else—foundation color, eye shadow, face powder, and liner pencils—she put back in the bag. She then carried the bag into the bathroom and set it on the floor behind a chintz curtain that wrapped around the bathroom sink to hide the basin's ancient plumbing.

Next came the two pieces of luggage Katherine had carried up from the car the night before. She dug about, separating cotton from silk, frilly lace bikini pants from thermal underwear, denim jeans from tailored slacks. Jeans, shirts, and sweaters went into the antique dresser by the bed. The rest was carelessly repacked and slipped under the bed in a kind of deliberate exile.

It was insane, but she felt defiant, even naughty, putting aside the expensive clothing and makeup that she used every day of her life to maintain the image of Katherine Mallory, actress. Chucking it all made her feel so good, it must be wicked. If it tastes bad and goes down hard, Katherine remembered hearing, the medicine was good for you. The reverse must also hold true, at least in this case.

Katherine giggled, unrepentant, and looked at herself in the mirror that hung over the dresser.

The glass was streaked and slightly fogged, but the image was clear. What she saw wasn't the carefully groomed, immaculately dressed Katherine she knew so well. And the stranger certainly wasn't the borderline floozy she created for *Bright Promise*'s Leanne Cameron. This female was without the hardness Katherine had somehow come to equate with her appearance. This lady's clear brown eyes were soft. Her pale hair shimmered straight to her shoulders, smooth and shining.

"K-K-K-Katie?" Katherine asked herself, peering close, as if expecting an answer.

By the time Katherine dressed and straightened up the cabin, she was beginning to feel a nagging ache in her stomach. She usually wasn't up and about for more than an hour before having breakfast. Feed me, her body demanded. Katherine pushed aside the thought and tried to concentrate on something else, on the blessed silence, and the way the sun was making its way through the open windows of the cabin and casting a warm glow over everything it touched.

It wasn't working. Katherine sighed and gave in. Changing all her habits in one day was probably too much to expect. She checked the utensil inventory in the kitchen and found she had everything she needed. Everything but food, and now that she had let herself go, Katherine was working up an enormous appetite. Well, it was only a few miles into the village, she reasoned, a good brisk walk. What better way to start the day?

Katherine dressed in jeans she had forgotten

were too tight, a long-sleeved western-style shirt, and high-topped boots with a low heel designed for long periods of wear. She tucked twenty dollars into the change pocket of her jeans—it was a struggle—and started out the door, arms swinging free.

As soon as she stepped outside the cabin, the winter sun washed over her. She debated a minute. The air was crisp but not too terribly cold. The thought of a jacket vanished from her mind. A deep breath took in the aroma of pine and cedar and the smell of wood burning in fireplaces and of breakfasts cooking on stoves in the houses that dotted the forest. The air was so clear, Katherine was sure she could smell bacon frying two miles away.

She looked up and shook her head in disbelief. Brilliant white cumulus clouds, like cotton puffs, exploded against a pale blue sky.

Katherine was humming as she set out along the winding path that led to the road toward Rimforest.

Her tune was quite different on the trek back to Flynn's Forest Retreat. Arms clasped around a loaded bag of groceries, Katherine hurried along the road. The sun had disappeared in the passing of an hour, eclipsed by dark, steadily moving clouds. Even the sky had changed from the placid blue of a baby's eyes to the sickly gray pallor of a mud puddle. Wind gusts ruffled the thin cotton of her shirt while the chill factor plunged.

Katherine shivered convulsively, hugging the grocery bag to her body for warmth. The road leading to the Retreat was on a barely perceptible incline, unless you were lugging ten pounds of coffee and eggs and trying to outsprint the wind. By the time she neared her destination, Katherine was blue-lipped and gasping for breath. The Retreat was just up ahead and she sagged with relief. If not for the sight of Joe Mercer's truck parked next to her car, Katherine's joy might have been complete. His Blazer was large and black, perched atop huge, wide tires, and it completely dwarfed the elegant lines of her Mercedes. The look of it, totally in tune with the surrounding landscape, brought home the conviction that Katherine was somehow out of place.

What had started out a beautiful day was quickly going downhill. Katherine broke stride for a moment as she neared the chalet office, gratified to see Joe was nowhere in sight to witness her defeat at the hands of the elements. Farther up the winding path, she noticed a young couple leaving their cabin snugly dressed for the weather, daypacks strapped to their backs. Katherine cast envious eyes on the girl's down-filled jacket and then stepped up her pace. The comfort of her cabin was only around the bend of the path.

As if purposely bedeviling her, Joe chose the moment Katherine was passing by the office to step out the door. He couldn't have timed it better if he had been lurking behind the drapes watching her struggle.

Unless she chose to be rude and ignore him altogether, Katherine had to acknowledge his presence. "Hi, Joe. How's the patient?" she called as she walked by, pointedly discouraging any conversation beyond a returned greeting. It was not only that she wholeheartedly wished to avoid speaking to Joe; she was beginning to shake so badly from the chill, she was sure her discomfort was visible.

"Better than you'll be if you don't start dressing warmer," Joe shot back. He didn't have the carefully trained eyes of a doctor for nothing.

Katherine blanched and stopped abruptly. "I happen to enjoy a good brisk walk. It's *very* stimulating," she retorted defensively.

"Sure." Smiling, he stepped in front of her. "But if you're really in to punishing yourself, why not try polar-bearing?"

Katherine sighed heavily, waiting. "Okay, I'll bite. What's polar-bearing?"

"Simple. Just throw yourself into Big Bear Lake in the dead of winter along with all the other masochists. It's a club," he explained gleefully. "They all line up on the shore in their bathing suits, somebody blows a whistle, and they plow into the water and start flapping around and probably wishing they were somewhere else. It only lasts a few minutes and then they all come out and bundle up and go home."

"Fascinating." Katherine smiled weakly. "Thanks for keeping me standing here, turning blue, while you shared that thrilling story with me."

"Hey," Joe protested, the picture of innocence. "I was just being friendly, trying to make up for last night. We did get off to a bad start." His tone suddenly lost its teasing quality. "You'd think two old friends would have better to say to each other after fifteen years. Here, you take this," he said as he slipped his jacket over Katherine's shoulders and reached for the bag of groceries, "and I'll take that."

Katherine stepped back, holding tight to the bag. "I can handle it, thanks."

"Come on, Katie," Joe whispered softly, "let me carry your books." He pried the bag loose and tucked it under one arm.

It was hard to maintain the proud thrust of her chin when her teeth were chattering like castanets. Besides, at that moment, she couldn't remember why after such a pleasant start they had become so testy with each other last night. And he seemed so eager to start again.

Katherine stopped resisting and thrust her arms into the jacket. Its fleece lining warmed her immediately, while a silly thought swept into her mind. If she were nine years old again, Katherine might have expected this kind of sweet, coaxing talk moments before Joe stuck a lizard down the front of her blouse. But she wasn't a child anymore and Joe didn't have his hands secreted behind his back and a cunning look on his face. So she was safe, wasn't she?

Katherine relaxed, laughing at her wild imagination. "All right," she acquiesced, "I surrender." The arms of the jacket hung four inches beyond her fingertips and she flip-flopped the cuffs toward Joe. "Let's start catching up. But you go first." She started walking slowly up the path, enjoying the feel of Joe's arm brushing against hers through the coat as he followed beside her.

"What do you want to know? How I made the transition from breaking into the Benedict house to becoming the village sawbones?" His reference to Katherine's flippant remarks the night before did not go unnoticed.

"That's a good place to start," Katherine agreed, refusing to allow irritation to boil up inside her. If memory served, Joe had never been known for his tact and diplomacy. What she might be quick to consider an abuse had probably not been intended in that manner. Anyway, she was determined to give Joe the benefit of the doubt. Why she felt so strongly about reestablishing a rapport between them, Katherine couldn't honestly say. She arched a delicate eyebrow and waited for Joe to continue.

"Actually, its pretty boring stuff." Joe shrugged, hunching his shoulders against the wind. "Hard work, long hours. I finished college in three years, then went on to med school, internship, residency, a few years' private practice." He shook his head as though dispelling the images his words brought to mind. "When Doc Taley decided to retire, I bought his practice and came home."

"Was it the right decision, coming back to Rimforest?" Katherine felt a bit cheated by Joe's nutshell description of the last decade, but sensed he wasn't willing to share more with her. She would have to content herself with skimpy bits and pieces of his life, for now.

"For me," he answered, "coming home was a matter of survival, really." He laughed harshly. "I was miserable in the city. Just a case of not being able to take the small-town boy out of the man, I suppose." Just when Katherine thought he was beginning to open up, Joe caught himself and fell quiet.

Still, she pressed on. "Are you married?" Even as she asked it, Katherine cringed inwardly, wondering if she sounded a little too interested in what the answer would be. She held her breath.

"I was, for about an hour." He showed no sign of pain in recalling the brief marriage. "Actually, it was more like eight months. No children, though, so I guess I was lucky it only lasted as long as it did. She was a city girl, born and bred. When I decided to come home, she thought I wanted to strand her on the moon." They were approaching the last cabin on the path. Joe stopped walking and turned to Katherine. "What about you? Any skeletons in your closet?"

"No." Katherine replied slowly. "Unlike the stereotypical Hollywood actress, I'm not divorced. But then, I've never been married, so it's been easy to beat the statistics."

"Ever come close?

Katherine shifted uneasily from one foot to another. "Yes, once." She tried for a lighter tone of voice than she felt. "Chris Massey," she said, expecting the name to evoke recognition from Joe. He gave her a blank look. "He's an actor," Katherine hastened to explain, hoping to cover her confusion. "At least he is now. He was just starting when I met him. Chris had a short-term contract with *Bright Promise* about five years ago. The show didn't pick up his option, so I did." She laughed humorlessly. "At first, we didn't marry because I was working and he wasn't. Then, when things started picking up for Chris ... Well, there was always something or other." All of a-sudden, Katherine wanted to put an end to the discussion of her less-than-fulfilling love affair. "Anyway, we just kept on finding one excuse after another, and pretty soon the gap between us got so wide someone else waltzed in and danced off with him." Katherine attempted a smile. "Divine justice, I suppose. I wouldn't settle for anything less than perfect, and that's just what they've got. Chris's wife is expecting their first child and he has his own prime-time show on Saturday nights." She frowned, remembering Chris's name had not sparked Joe's interest. "Don't you ever watch television?"

"Not much." He shrugged casually, as though he had no idea most Americans spent six hours a day glued to the tube. "I've seen you, of course. Every set in Rimforest is tuned to *Bright Promise* during the afternoons. Whenever I make a house call, I have to do my doctoring during the station breaks." Joe stopped in front of the steps leading to Katherine's cabin. "I don't suppose you could get the sponsors to make their commercials a bit longer, could you?"

Katherine laughed. "Not likely! I can tell you're not an ardent fan. Most viewers would boycott a soap if there were any more commercials. As it is, they get only about seventeen actual minutes of story for every half-hour of television time."

"Well, it was just a thought." Joe grinned. "Sure would make my job easier. Speaking of which, I have another call to make and then some office appointments until two o'clock. How 'bout if I come back here when I'm done and take you out for a late lunch?" As though he thought he needed

an added incentive to persuade her, Joe added
hastily, "I could show you around if you like."

"I'm hardly a tourist, Joe," Katherine reminded
him, aware of a sudden tightness in her chest.

Joe gave her an exasperated nod. "*I* didn't say
that, you did. Look, Katie, I don't want to get
into another . . . Do you want to have lunch with
me or not?"

"Yes." Katherine realized she had been holding her breath, and exhaled it in a long, tremulous sigh. "Yes, I do," she said forcibly, slipping
out of Joe's jacket and handing it back to him in
exchange for her groceries. "I'll be waiting. Good-
bye, Joe."

Katherine couldn't muster enough energy to
pull herself off the bed for another hour. What
with the exhausting uphill walk and Joe's impli-
cation that she was a stranger in her own hometown, Katherine felt nearly done in, and it wasn't
even noon yet. She didn't need this on the very
first morning of her vacation! Still, as much as
she would have liked to avoid it, Katherine was
faced with some hard, cold facts and she had Joe
Mercer to thank for setting the gears of her brain
in motion.

She hadn't come back for the reunion, not really.
Not that she didn't remember or care about the
seventy-two other members of her graduating
class, but she hadn't kept in touch because cut-
ting all the ties with Rimforest and concentrating on her new life in Los Angeles was easier.
And as long as she was being brutally truthful
with herself, nothing else had been more impor-

tant at the time she left than being an actress, and she would have sacrificed her childhood, her future, *anything*, to obtain her goal. So she told herself that Mother was right. How could she hope to be a success if she spent all her time mooning over the friends and places she had left behind? After a few years, the faces had become blurred and she had a hard time recalling the last names of teachers and whether you turned right or left on Sky Drive to get to the trout stream behind the old Miller place. And it was . . . it was less complicated that way. Katherine forgot more and more each year, until the pain of it diminished. Forgot about it until the glitter of her new life got so bright she felt compelled to turn her eyes away and look again at the place of her uncomplicated youth.

Why was she now so desperate to recapture it all? Was she really so unhappy with what she had that the people and moments she'd lost could take on such importance? Whatever her motivation, Katherine was sure of one thing: she had to find a place where she could put the frantic pace of her life into perspective. A place where she could relax and come to grips with herself. True, she could have picked any one of a hundred places, but something had brought her back to Rimforest. Here she had chosen to find herself again.

With that thought paramount in her mind, Katherine fixed a belated breakfast, amazed at how quickly she devoured the food on her plate. She had very little experience in the kitchen, but the eggs and bacon she prepared tasted like the finest gourmet meal at the Polo Lounge in Beverly Hills. Even the coffee, hot and strong, went down like Dom Perignon. She was more than a little pleased with her efforts.

After breakfast, Katherine checked her watch and found she still had three hours before Joe would be back. She decided to put on a sweater and go out onto the porch. The rest of the morning would be spent lounging in a rocker with her feet up on the railing. And she would try, try very hard, not to analyze her motives for returning to Rimforest. Soul-searching was all very well, but at the same time, too much of it was damn boring. There was nothing worse than a whiner, and that was exactly what she was fast becoming. If the sky opened up and a shattering insight was delivered by way of a crackling thunderbolt, fine! But she wasn't going to keep brooding. She was back in her hometown for a short visit, pure and simple. And right now she was going to lean back, relax, and pass the morning trying to identify the various forms of wildlife scurrying around in the trees beyond the porch. Then, in a few hours' time, a handsome doctor was coming to take her out. *That* surprising development was enough to contemplate.

"I should have known you'd bring me here." Katherine giggled and shook her head helplessly after the waitress took their order and retreated into the kitchen. They had missed the lunch crowd, but the café hadn't changed much since the days when it had been filled to capacity with the kids from her own graduating class.

"This is new for me, too," Joe said, raising his brows in protest. "I haven't been back in years. But the kids still hang out here, so I figure nothing has changed."

"Well, as long as we're tripping down memory lane,"—Katherine pointed to a corner booth on the other side of the room—"isn't that where you and your friends held court after school? The girls on this side, the boys over there, and Joe Mercer the absolute last word in protocol. I can see you now"—her hands formed a make-believe television screen—"sitting there in your letterman's jacket, sandwiched between two adoring females. But, of course, you ignore them and concentrate on planning the evening's hell-raising with . . . ah, let's see . . . Willie Carpenter and Hal O'Neal. Am I right?"

"Is that how you remember it?" Joe asked incredulously. "Because if it is, there must have been someone else wandering around Rimforest with my face. I was *never* here in the afternoons. I worked for Doc Taley every day after school, Saturdays too. You must have me confused with some other Joe Mercer."

"Oh, come on," Katherine coaxed, "I can't be that far wrong. Besides, you're nit-picking. So it wasn't after school, it was during lunch break, but one way or another, you and your cronies were the big fish in our little pool. But I didn't know you worked for Doc Taley," she admitted. "Is that how you got interested in medicine?"

"Yes, in a roundabout sort of way." Joe paused

a moment as the waitress brought two cups of coffee. "I started working for him because it was the only job available at the time and I needed the money for dates and to keep my car on the streets. Let's see, I guess I was sixteen. My dad and Doc Taley were fishing buddies, so I'd been around him and his office most of my life. But I was never one of those kids who bandaged everybody in the neighborhood or brought home stray dogs to fix them up. Doc must have seen something in me I didn't even know was there. By the time I graduated, he had me doing things that might have cost him his license, and I was good and royally hooked." He grinned affectionately and Katherine was struck by how really blue Joe's eyes were and how little lines were beginning to crease at the ends of his lids because he smiled so much. "My folks moved to Victorville later that year," he continued, unaware of her scrutiny, "so I stayed with Doc while I did my premed in Pomona. Later I came back to help out during summer breaks while I was at Stanford. Anyway, you already know the rest. It worked out that I came home for good."

"You said you took over for Doc Taley?" Katherine asked. "Where is he now?"

"He moved down to a retirement community in Riverside," Joe answered with obvious regret. "I visit him on Sundays, but it's just not the same anymore."

He was so quiet suddenly that Katherine was at a loss as to what to say to him. Mercifully the waitress solved the problem by setting down two plates of hamburgers and french fires in front of them.

Katherine bit into the hamburger and chewed it slowly, anticipating the fondly remembered tastes and smells. Her eyes widened, and then she and Joe both started to chuckle at the same time.

Joe swallowed hard, grimacing. "Do you think the burgers were as bad as this fifteen years ago and we just weren't smart enough to know it?"

"I don't know." Katherine gave him a quizzical smile. "But there must be a lesson to be learned here. Nothing's ever quite as good as you remember it?"

Something moved beneath the sky blue of Joe's eyes as he reached across the table and took her hand. "Oh, I don't know about that. But, come on, let's get out of here. There's a sandwich shop down by my office, and while the atmosphere doesn't conjure up images of letterman sweaters and days gone by, at least the food is edible."

Once they were resituated and eating the avocado-and-bean-sprout sandwiches on wheat bread that Joe assured her were better for them anyway, Katherine fell into the time-honored tradition of asking after the other members of their graduating class.

Connie Jaimet? Married Bill George and moved to Orange County. Willie Carpenter? Has his own architectural business in Moonridge, outside of Big Bear. Hal O'Neal? In the business of refurbishing cabins and then reselling them at a profit. Ellin Mayjors? Moved to Colorado.

"Some have stayed on," Joe told her, "but most have either moved away or . . . Well, you'll see, at the reunion. We had a pretty big turnout five years ago. Fifty out of seventy-two. I expect it'll be about the same this year." He checked the time and then called for the check. "What the hell is wrong with her?" Joe grumbled when the waitress hung back, giggling and whispering to the other girl who worked in the sandwich shop. "Oh, it's *you*! I'd almost forgotten I'm in the presence of a celebrity. Christ, how do you stand it? All that nudging and pointing. How do you get anything done?"

"It isn't so bad, at least not usually," Katherine objected mildly. "It would be worse if I was in movies. Although you know, for some reason people feel more comfortable about a television actress, especially a soap star. It's almost as though they see you every day, good and bad, crying and laughing and scheming, chewing up the scenery, and it's like they know you intimately. You don't have the same mystique as a movie star. You're more like a comfortable old shoe. Anyway, I've found that the more you play at being a star, the more your privacy is taken away. I gave up wearing dark glasses and sloping hats long ago. You'd be surprised," she teased gently, "but whole days pass without my being mobbed. Now, if you'll stop drawing so much attention to us and just pay the bill, I think we can get out of here with a minimum of fanfare."

On the way back to the Retreat, Joe detoured along Bear Springs Road to Strawberry Peak Lookout—a favorite parking spot for young lovers—past Katherine's old house on Blackfoot Trail and the church she used to attend on Grass Valley Road. They fell into a comfortable silence and she was almost painfully disappointed when he braked to a stop in front of her cabin.

"I'm going to be busy the rest of the weekend," he told her without apology. "You have any plans for Monday night? Dinner?"

"I'd love to, Joe." Katherine stood next to him on the porch, smiling up at him. "And thanks for this afternoon."

"My pleasure," he said huskily, his hand resting gently on her shoulder. For a moment it seemed as though he was going to kiss her, but then he straightened slightly, as though catching himself.

"Why, Joe," Katherine whispered, wanting him to follow his first impulse, "were you thinking of kissing me here in broad daylight, in front of God and everybody?"

His answer was the kiss she had been hoping for, soft and light, brushing over her lips with an almost agonizing sweetness. Katherine was stunned by her own clinging response. She was just doing a little innocent flirting—wasn't she?—and suddenly she was weak in the knees, dazed by the tremor that shook through her body like an earthquake.

"I knew it!" Joe murmured against her mouth before he let her go. "You couldn't possibly play

Leanne Cameron so well if there wasn't a touch of wildness beneath that cool, proper exterior." He winked and landed a playful kiss on the tip of her nose. "See you Monday night."

Chapter Three

❦

The next morning, Katherine lay in bed under a thick, fluffy quilt and recited the reasons why she should get up and out of bed. There were places to go, people to see. She was hungry and her mouth felt like queer fuzzy things had taken up permanent residence. Oh, but it was so warm and toasty under the quilt, and she knew that once the cold air of the cabin slipped inside her nightgown she would be shaking and shivering for an hour until the wood she had to start in the fireplace began to warm up the place.

But someone had to do it and this sure wasn't the Beverly Hills Hotel. There was no button she could press for service, no one else to depend on for her comforts but herself. Her agent, Larry Michaels, had suggested the Arrowhead Lodge. They, at least, had central heating, but no, Katherine wouldn't hear of it. She wanted to rough it, to recreate her girlhood as closely as possible. Now she wondered if her stubbornness was a symptom of total mental collapse. What she wouldn't do for carpeted floors, a restaurant just off the lobby, and room service at this moment!

Groaning, Katherine tested the air with a hesitant foot poked out from beneath the quilt. Courage, my girl, she told herself as she leaped from the bed and ran toward the woodpile beside the fireplace.

Breakfast this morning tasted even better than the day before. She must be getting the hang of it. Before long, she'd be able to add bacon and eggs to her limited prowess in the kitchen. How did anyone live thirty-two years without knowing just how long it took to fry an egg over-medium?

Katherine showered and dressed warmly before cleaning up the breakfast dishes and straightening the cabin. She had forgotten to wind her watch the night before, but judging from the light outside the window and the distant sound of cars moving about near the office, the hour was ripe for civilized people to be up and about.

Before leaving the cabin, Katherine pulled on a caramel-colored blazer over the pale blue sweater she was already wearing. She was determined not to be caught underdressed again. She had considered buying one of those down-filled parkas, but somehow, as slim and tall as she was, she still would have felt like the Pillsbury doughboy and she wasn't yet willing to sacrifice style completely for warmth.

Katherine shut the door behind her and walked down the path to her car. The engine of the Mercedes turned over without too much protest and she backed out of the gravel driveway and headed toward the village.

As she drove, her thoughts drifted reluctantly to Joe. He was most probably on his way down

the mountain at that very moment, going into
Riverside to visit Doc Taley. Did he spend the
entire day with Doc, or would he be on his way
back in the afternoon? How did he spend the
rest of his Sundays?

Impatiently Katherine pushed the questions
from her mind. She had no more intention of
dwelling on Joe than she had of trying to solve
the other problems in her life. Problems? Now,
why should she think of him in that vein? She
wasn't going to be around long enough for anything between them to develop into a problem.
She was attracted to Joe with an intensity she
hadn't felt about any man for a long time, but a
simple physical response was not a commitment
for life. Besides, he fell under the title of unfinished business. Perhaps that was his main attraction. Seeing him again stirred up all sorts of
fantasies and thoughts. Naturally, she wondered
what it would have been like, how it would have
felt to . . .

She had reached the mini-Swiss chalet that
housed the Shea Real Estate office. The building
was pink with white scallops on the pointed roof
that resembled snow. It looked more like a ginger-
bread house than a real-estate office, but one
place was as good as the next for Katherine's
purposes. She wanted to look into the possibility
of purchasing a vacation home. A place far removed from the pressures of her life in Los
Angeles.

Katherine parked and walked to the door of
the office. As she opened it, a cow bell thudded
dully in her ear and she shut the door behind

her. The office was empty, but a voice called out from beyond the small room that held two desks. Pictures of homes and bare lots littered the walls of the office, and Katherine viewed each one with the interest of a prospective buyer. The woman's voice called out again, instructing Katherine to make herself comfortable and asking if she wanted a cup of coffee.

Katherine refused politely and sat down to wait. In a few minutes, a woman came rushing in, breathless from the exertion of moving about. She was *very* pregnant, at least eight months, Katherine observed just as she directed her gaze to the woman's face.

"Janet!" Katherine screamed happily. She stood up to give the woman an affectionate hug.

"I heard you were coming back, Katie, but I didn't think to see you until next week." Janet hugged her again, then stood back. "Girl, you haven't changed a bit. I hate you." Janet patted her enormous stomach. "My first. And I show up at the reunion looking like a blimp."

"Andy Shea." Katherine connected the name outside with Janet's condition. "You married Andy Shea."

"Six years ago." Janet sighed happily. "I have to sit down, Katie." She maneuvered her body into a chair behind the desk. "This little monster weighs a ton."

Katherine took a chair opposite Janet, grinning senselessly. It was so nice to be welcomed back with the feeling that she had hardly been away. Janet Willin. Janet Shea, now. She looked marvelous. Pregnancy agreed with her, bringing out a glow in her dark skin and black eyes. Katherine paused, remembering Andy Shea. He and Janet were both large-boned and tall, but Andy was as fair as Janet was dark. How interesting to see the baby the two of them would produce.

"Gosh, it's good to see you, Katie." Janet beamed at her like a doting aunt. "You know, I watch you on *Bright Promise* whenever I can. You're just great. That Leanne Cameron is one sleazy bitch."

"Thanks, Janet." Katherine laughed with her. "I try."

"So, what brings you here?" Janet asked. "You sure weren't expecting to see me when you walked through the door. Your eyes almost fell out of your head."

"That's right," Katherine agreed. "I came in to have someone show me what's for sale in the area, but it looks like I'll have to wait for Andy."

"Are you kidding?" Janet replied, clearly astonished that anyone would consider her condition a delicate one. "I'll be showing property up until the minute they wheel me into the delivery room." She chuckled contentedly and stood up. "When you run a mom-and-pop store, you can't afford to let anything get by you. Look, I'll make a deal with you. You come out to dinner with Andy and me tonight and I'll show you my best property, okay? I may even let you buy one." Janet reached for a large notebook and flipped it open. "Now, what are you looking for?"

Katherine pondered the question for a moment. "A lot of things." Her voice caught with emotion.

"But, for the time being, I'll settle for a sweet little cottage that feels like home."

At seven that evening, Katherine parked outside the Rimview Inn, where she was meeting the Sheas for dinner. Before she went inside, she checked her image in the car mirror and ran a comb through her pale hair. Of all the strange sensations she'd experienced since arriving in Rimforest, this was the oddest. The Rimview Inn had always been a place for "grown-ups" to drink and dance, and in the eyes of adolescents who were too young to pass through its doors, it acquired an almost legendary glamour. Katherine had left Rimforest long before her twenty-first birthday and so the Rimview Inn had remained mysterious and unapproachable in her mind.

And now here she was, at last, acutely aware that she had left Rimforest a child and was returning a woman. Katherine smiled at the thought and got out of the car, bracing against the cold night wind for a short dash to the door.

Inside, the Rimview had the look of a 1940's roadhouse. It was very dark and the walls were cluttered with framed pictures of the owner, now deceased, in the company of sport and screen celebrities who had stopped at the inn on their way up and down the mountain. Off to the right was a large open-beamed dining room with candles on each linen-covered table. To the left, behind double doors that swung open on hinges, was the bar and dancing area. Both well over six feet tall, Janet and Andy Shea were not difficult to find. Katherine simply looked over the heads of the other diners and zeroed in on them easily.

The Rimview was famous locally for its prime rib. The food was delicious, the wine complementary, and the talk easy and comfortable. Katherine adroitly steered the conversation away from herself. Beyond answering a few questions about her daily schedule while filming *Bright Promise,* she expressed a greater interest in real-estate prices and creative financing and was rewarded for her persistence when the Sheas got caught up in her enthusiasm and began talking about the subject dearest to their hearts.

They had just finished their meal and were preparing to go into the dance area for an after-dinner drink when the first of three women approached Katherine asking for her autograph. The interludes were brief and friendly but Katherine couldn't help but laugh at the look of astonishment on Janet's face.

"Don't worry," Katherine assured her with a grin while slipping an arm through Janet's and walking away from the table, "there's no danger of the baby becoming a soap-opera fan through osmosis."

"Worry," Janet sputtered, trying to keep her voice low. "I think it's great! My God, don't you just love it? Imagine!" She feigned a pout and shrugged. "The only time I get to sign my name is on escrow papers."

Andy patted Janet affectionately and asked Katherine if she was often ogled and pointed out in a crowd.

"Yes and no," Katherine answered as honestly

as she could. "It depends, really. I've never done a feature film so it's not as though I'm instantly recognizable, outside of being an actress on a daytime soap. Sometimes it's more a chain-reaction kind of thing. You know, one person knowing who I am and then someone else asking for an autograph because the first person did. I once had a man tell me he had no idea what I did but if it was important to the lady that just left the table he wasn't going to take any chances and pass me by."

The moment Andy pushed open the swinging doors to the dance area, they were hit by a blast of twanging, raucous country music from a six-man band playing on a platform in the corner of the large barnlike room. Small tables—the kind where everyone's knees bang together underneath—edged a solid oak dance floor, and a frantically busy bar ran the entire length of one wall.

Andy grabbed one hand of each woman and guided them through the crowd to one of the tables farthest away from the loudspeakers. On the floor, couples were dancing, and, from the look of it, having a marvelous time.

Katherine hardly knew what to make of the noise and smoke and the shoulder-to-shoulder press of warm bodies. Not that Los Angeles wasn't riddled with country-western bars. But Katherine and her friends were more into candlelit dinners at Ma Maison and theater nights at the Dorothy Chandler Pavilion.

Within ten minutes the sweater Katherine was wearing had become too weighty for the oppressive heat in the room. She leaned back in her chair and pulled it off, revealing a soft apricot-colored silk blouse that did wonders for the highlights of her ivory-hued skin and dark eyes.

Andy came back from the bar with their drinks, and while she sat sipping a tumbler of bourbon neat, Katherine gave up the idea of pleasant after-dinner conversation and joined the Sheas in watching the dancers. From the way Janet's feet were tapping, Katherine knew that if it wasn't for the cumbersome, out-of-kilter balance of her body, Janet and Andy would be out on the floor in an instant. Occasionally one or the other would lean across the table and yell something of interest, but by and large, the next hour was spent in people-watching. Katherine was getting tired of having to explain that she wasn't familiar with the steps to the men who came up and asked her to dance, but she loved the whole atmosphere of the place and made a mental note to be better prepared the next time she came.

By the time ten o'clock rolled around Katherine could barely keep her eyes open despite the loud music and frenetic activity surrounding her. The long day, high altitude, and two drinks after dinner all combined to put her into a lethargy that almost lulled her to sleep where she sat.

She was preparing to make her excuses to the Sheas and drive back to the cabin when the arrival of a couple three tables to the right drew a chorus of hoots and cheers. Katherine's head swiveled at the sound and she found herself watching as Joe pulled back a chair and held it for one of the most beautiful women Katherine had ever seen. The woman sat, and as Joe started to move around her, she put her hand on his arm and drew him close to whisper something in his ear that caused him to laugh.

Katherine felt her stomach turn over, and a heated flush spread to her cheeks. As much as she wanted to, she couldn't pull her eyes away. Frozen like stone, she watched as Joe sat next to the woman and allowed himself to be pawed in a totally distasteful public display.

The woman was all over him, covering his hand with her own, leaning against his arm, brushing back a few stray strands of his thick hair.

Katherine's jaw clenched so tightly her chin began to ache. She was seized with an irrational desire to march over to the woman and snarl, "If you don't stop mauling this man, I'm going to rip your arm out of the socket and beat you over the head with it!"

Instead, she decided the best course to take was one of retreat. Her unexpected and embarrassingly childish jealousy did have one advantage, though. The surge of adrenaline going up her back instilled just enough raw energy to make certain she'd stay awake on the drive back to the cabin and not run the car off a cliff or wrap it around a tree.

"Janet?" Katherine stood and folded her sweater over her arm. "I'd better call it a night. It's been a long fourteen hours and I'm exhausted. Andy, thanks so much for dinner. It was lovely." She touched Janet's shoulder lightly. "I'll see you Tuesday for some more house-hunting, okay? Good night."

She probably should have gone the long way

around the room and avoided the chance that Joe
would look up and see her, but after giving the
idea fleeting consideration, Katherine opted to
leave Rimview Inn the same way she had entered.
Besides, she wanted him to see her, wanted him
to be aware that she was undaunted by the knowl-
edge that he was out with a stunning young
woman twenty-four hours after he had stood on
the cabin porch with Katherine and kissed her
tenderly.

She pretended surprise when the inevitable
happened and Joe called her name, raising a hand
to wave her over to the table. While she listened
to the even, slightly amused tone of Joe's voice,
Katherine's veiled interest rested solely with the
woman he was introducing.

Pamela Jaimet. Connie Jaimet's younger sister.
She was gorgeous. Cool green eyes and natural
auburn hair the shade most women spent hun-
dreds of dollars and hours under the hands of a
stylist to achieve. And there was nothing kid-
sisterish about her body, which she was pressing
so tightly against Joe she seemed to want to dis-
solve under his skin.

Standing there, Katherine instantly regretted
her hasty decision. She should have gone the
long way around and avoided this altogether. What
was she going to have to blunder into before she
realized that not every scene was scripted in her
favor? Leanne Cameron, without an ounce of
shame or decency, would have played this well,
but Katherine Mallory was already starting to
cringe. With a great effort, she forced a weak
smile to her lips when Pamela insisted she join

them, if only for a few minutes. Joe, damn him, appeared completely unperturbed by the fact that Katherine was taking a seat across the table from him.

"Joe was just telling me you'd come back for the reunion. I know you probably hear this a lot, but I think you're a marvelous actress. Oh, look at Joe." Pamela laughed gaily. "He's giving me his most serious and reprimanding 'doctor' expression. I told him if he'd introduce us, I wouldn't act like a star-struck kid, and here I am babbling away first thing about . . . Oh, well, I'll change the subject." Pam flashed a genuinely friendly smile. "My sister Connie and her husband, Bill, are going to be staying with me for the reunion. I hope you'll come for dinner one night. Joe"—there went those casually possessive fingers to his arm again—"almost everyone is coming up for at least the weekend, some for the entire week. Why don't we get everybody together for a potluck at my place?" She turned to Katherine. "You'll come, won't you?"

"Yes, of course," Katherine choked. What a depressing idea! She'd have to come up with a good excuse at the last minute, but she would sooner enjoy a long evening alone than watch Joe and Pamela cavort all evening long.

While Pamela chattered merrily on, blithely ignoring the fact that no one else was able to squeeze a word in edgewise, Katherine squirmed in her chair, hoping Pam would take a breath soon so that she could say she had to be going back to the Retreat. For all the nonstop talking, Pam seemed a nice-enough young woman. She was certainly pretty enough to turn any man's head.

If he can get past that constant babble, Katherine thought, giving in to a touch of bitchiness. Still, it was almost impossible not to warm to Pam's enthusiasm. But Joe ... Well, instead of being even the slightest bit embarrassed, he seemed to be enjoying himself immensely. He didn't even have the good manners to hide the devilish gleam in his eyes when he looked from Pamela to Katherine and back again.

"We're never going to get a drink, waiting for the waitress to come to the table," Pam complained good-naturedly. "Someone is going to have to go over to the bar. No, don't get up," she said teasingly as she stood and patted Joe's shoulder when he made no move to rise. "I'll do it. I see someone over there I want to talk to anyway. Can I get you something, Katherine?"

At last! The opening she was waiting for. Katherine declined, murmured the standard amenities, and got to her feet as Pam hurried off in the direction of the bar.

"Not so fast, Katie." Joe reached out and took her arm, tilting his head to indicate the band's change in tempo to a slow dance. "They're playing our song."

Katherine allowed herself to be guided onto the dance floor. "I've *never* heard this song before," she scoffed gently.

"Neither have I," Joe admitted, "but I have it on the best authority that this very song was played the night of our senior prom, so, in a way, you still owe me this dance."

Katherine's first impulse was to remind Joe that he had come to the Rimview in the company of another woman, but then his arm slipped around her waist and his other hand felt so warm as it closed over her stiff fingers. The top of her head fit snugly under his chin and she rested her cheek lightly on the soft wool of his shirt.

"You smell good, Katie," he whispered against her hair, drawing her tighter with each beat of the music. "Even when you were a kid, you always smelled good, like you just stepped out of a bathtub." He laughed softly, almost to himself, and the hand he held at her back moved slowly up until it touched the tips of her hair and his fingers curled around the soft, silky tresses.

"I was just as grubby as any other little girl," Katherine protested in a voice that bore no resemblance to her usual cool tones. If only he wasn't holding her so closely and whispering so warmly in her ear. If only his hand would stop brushing lightly over her back and just stay in one place. She couldn't seem to get enough air into her lungs in the normal manner and so she was breathing through her mouth.

This was crazy. It was just one simple little dance and she was reacting as if they were alone together in some secluded corner of the world. Every nerve in her body was tingling and straining. Her heart was hammering so hard in her chest she wondered if he could feel it thudding through the silk of her blouse.

"No," Joe alluded huskily to her last reply, "you were never like other little girls. I remember how it used to astonish me that you never seemed to get ruffled and dirty. You were always so starched and proper."

Katherine could hear it in his voice and feel it in the way their bodies fit together: Joe wasn't any better off than she was; he was having the same trouble keeping up the pretense of casual conversation. She laughed softly. "It appears neither of us has a very dependable memory when it comes to our childhood, but if I really looked so prissy to you, maybe you should have tried to put a few wrinkles in my dress."

"I *did* try." Joe's hand cupped her chin and lifted Katherine's face so that she was looking into his eyes as they swayed to the music. "Don't you remember all the times I chased you and teased you? The times I acted like a fool to get your attention? Or"—his mouth lowered, brushing gently across her cheek—"the night we were together at the Benedict cabin?"

Katherine was just about to answer when she looked toward the edge of the dance floor and saw Pamela watching them closely. She was holding two drinks in her hands and the friendly smile had given way to a look of stunned surprise and betrayal. Katherine stiffened guiltily and pulled away from Joe, murmuring a hasty good night before weaving her way through the crowd and off the dance floor to the exit beyond.

On the drive back to the Retreat, Katherine had a hard time keeping her mind on the twists and turns of the road. Both she and Joe were to blame for letting their mutual attraction get out of hand. There was really no excuse for hurting Pamela's feelings in such a thoughtless manner.

And yet, the woman had no ring on her finger, a stronger, more ruthless voice reminded Katherine. It was every woman for herself. If Joe had some previous commitment to Pamela, Katherine reasoned, he wouldn't have been so easily lured away.

Oh, you're getting good at this, she sighed as she neared the turnoff for the Retreat. Doesn't take long at all to think up convenient excuses for your behavior, to justify anything as long as it suits your purposes.

Katherine shuddered at the obvious comparison. Just like Leanne.

That she awoke the next morning stiff and sore and sporting the granddaddy of all headaches came as no surprise to Katherine. She'd had a miserable night, tossing from one side to another, punching holes the size of coconuts in her pillow, trying to find a comfortable position, and, for all her concentrated efforts, she'd gotten perhaps three hours' sleep.

She groaned, holding her head between two hands as she scrambled to the bathroom to riffle through her makeup case. No aspirin. A thousand dollars' worth of specially blended creams and lotions and not one ninety-cent bottle of aspirin!

Brushing her teeth was a chore Katherine was desperate to perform, but as soon as she was done she threw on some clothes in a haphazard fashion and stumbled out the door in the direction of the main office. Molly Flynn was bound to have a few aspirin, and Katherine was determined to ferret them out.

She was almost growling when she turned the corner to the front office and, indeed, that sound erupted from her throat as she came to a lurching halt at the sight of Molly and Joe seated on the porch sharing a cup of morning coffee.

"What are you doing here?" Katherine snapped testily, raising a hand to shade her throbbing eyes from the glare of the sun.

Molly looked from one to the other and burst out laughing. "That's what I was just asking! I told Doc Mercer that I was just fine when he called earlier, but here he is anyway." She snickered dotingly as she got up and started to walk inside the office. "And I don't flatter myself it's on account of an old lady's bronchitis."

The screen door slammed shut behind her and the sound of it raised the hairs at the back of Katherine's neck. She sighed heavily and sagged against the porch railing.

"You look awful." Joe uttered the understatement of the century without much sympathy. "Hung-over?"

"No," Katherine moaned impatiently. "I have a headache, that's all. I didn't sleep very well last night."

"Well"—Joe grinned happily—"I hope it had something to do with me." He opened his medical bag and retrieved several capsules. "Take two of these and *I'll* call you in the afternoon." Seeing he wasn't going to get much response, Joe colored slightly and admitted rather sheepishly, "That's really why I came out this morning. I wanted to find out if we could meet earlier than we'd originally planned. Say, about three? We'll still have dinner, but there's something I want to show you first."

Katherine plucked the capsules from his open palm. "If I'm not dead, I'll be waiting at three o'clock for the revelation. 'Bye." Without another word or a glance behind her, Katherine turned back to her cabin.

She took the pills, washed down with a glass of orange juice, and crawled back into bed, pulling the covers up over her head. This headache wasn't kidding around. She could only hope that Doc Mercer's magic-elixir pills would do their stuff and get her on her feet by three o'clock. As badly as her head pounded and as wildly as her stomach was flopping around, Katherine fell back to sleep thinking how handsome Joe had looked sitting there on the porch in his snug, faded jeans and a heavy wool Rob Roy tartan jacket.

At two o'clock she finally woke up again, and after lying on the bed for five minutes to test whether or not the headache was gone, Katherine rolled gingerly from under the quilt. The first order of business was getting something, anything, into her stomach. Another glass of orange juice and a piece of toast was about all she could manage, but it did seem to settle in nicely. After a leisurely shower, Katherine let her hair dry naturally and turned her attention to what she would wear.

If the past two days were any indication of his intent, then what Joe had to show her almost certainly had nothing to do with fancy restaurants—or anything indoors, for that matter. Katherine decided to forgo glamour in favor of comfort and practicality, choosing fur-lined boots and warm clothes. Still, she wasn't too displeased with the outcome. Her bulky-knit ski sweater was the color of burnished copper, and its warm Shetland wool was handsomely knit in an all-over cable stitch.

Because she had dallied so long, Katherine only had time to stuff her hair up under a tweed cap before she went to answer Joe's knock on the door.

Beyond telling her that she looked greatly improved since the early morning, Joe was quiet and pensive as he walked her to his truck and helped her in.

Almost, Katherine thought uneasily, as though something had happened to change his mind about her. Why that should upset her to any large degree was a thought guaranteed to start another band of little men armed with pickaxes working on her temples again.

The drive took them fifteen minutes out of Rimforest to a badly paved road overlooking Lake Gregory. There, on Montreaux Drive, between two large, expensive mountain homes, an expansive house was in the last stages of construction. The driveway was leveled out but not cemented, there were chalk marks still on the glass windows, and, inside, the hardwood floors had yet to be oiled and varnished and the walls were still unfinished plasterboard. Still, it was going to be beautiful. The entire north wall of the house's top level was glassed and offered a panoramic view of the placid lake below, and a wooden deck ran the length of the house outside the sliding glass doors. Katherine remembered that no motorboats were allowed on the lake, so even in summer the setting would be peaceful and uncluttered except for an occasional paddleboat or lakeside fisherman.

Joe gave her the complete tour. Three bedrooms, kitchen, living area, dining room, and two baths on the top level. An enormous family room, another bedroom and bath, and a small office on the lower.

"It's a bit on the large side for me now," Joe admitted with a shrug, "but I'm building it for a lifetime and I figure to have other people living in it with me someday."

"You're building?" Katherine repeated. "You mean you did all this yourself?"

"Most of it. I told an architect what I wanted and had him draw up the plans, and someone else laid the foundation, but the rest has taken me over a year of weekends and Wednesday afternoons. Another month and I'll be ready to move in."

"It's beautiful," Katherine said wistfully, thinking of her own stark, modern apartment. "I especially like that fireplace." She pointed to the west wall and a fireplace that was almost large enough to walk into, made of huge rocks and massive wooden beams.

"Ah, my pride and joy!" Joe walked over to the fireplace and ran a hand over its jagged surface. "This baby took me three months to build, but it was worth it."

"Wouldn't it have been easier if you'd brought some friends in to help you?"

"No. I wanted to do it on my own." Joe turned back and smiled like a little boy about to reveal a secret. "I bought this land when I was seventeen, out of the money I earned working for Doc. A hundred and fifty dollars down and twenty-three dollars a month. You know, there were times during med school and my internship when even that was hard to come up with, but I did it. I never stopped thinking about the house I wanted to build here someday. This place has been my own private Xanadu. I didn't want to share it with anyone else."

"Are you trying to tell me that Pamela hasn't picked out the curtains yet?" Katherine couldn't resist the jibe.

"Pam's got nothing to do with my house," Joe retorted uncomfortably. "She's a friend, that's all."

And that was all he was going to say about it. Joe's tone implied that a full explanation wasn't really due Katherine, and she had to admit he was right. After all, the two of them weren't at a point in their relationship when picking out a silver and china pattern was a pressing consideration. And, God willing, they never would be. Katherine wasn't looking for a lifetime commitment, especially with an unsophisticated backwoods doctor. There was no room in her life for that sort of complication. All she wanted was a little romance along with her two-week vacation. Why was she hanging back, looking for imaginary obstacles to overcome, setting up subtle conditions before getting on to the business of a casual affair she had already decided to enter into? From the moment Joe had led her out to the dance floor of the Rimview Inn, from the first touch of his hand encircling her waist and the feel of his mouth lingering against her skin, Katherine had known he was precisely the diversion she needed.

The lengthy silence between them was casting a pall over what had started out as a pleasant afternoon together. Katherine took a deep breath and walked over to stand beside Joe. "Is it really true that no one has ever been here before?" Her hand rested on his shoulder as he nodded silently. "Well, I like your house, Joe, and I'm glad I was your first guest." She kissed him lightly. "Thank you."

Joe's arms went around her waist and drew her tightly against him as his mouth lowered on hers again. He kissed her, a long, tender kiss, and when he let her go, Katherine was reeling. To her horror, she realized her reaction had nothing to do with Joe's expertise. She swallowed hard to fight back the rolling sensation in her stomach, a dizziness that left her shaky and breathless. Moaning helplessly, protesting the inconvenience, she sagged against Joe for support.

"Oh, Joe," she whispered into his shirt, "I hate to spoil this, but if I don't get something to eat soon, I'm going to faint."

Joe's hands went to her shoulders and then guided Katherine to the stone ledge of the fireplace, where he sat her down.

"That stupid headache this morning was so

bad I couldn't keep anything down but a piece of toast and a few sips of orange juice," she explained. "Now I'm hungry. I'm not used to going all day without eating."

"You city women are a fainthearted lot." Joe chuckled softly. "Wait here. I'll be right back."

He was gone before Katherine had a chance to speak. In the distance she heard him going into the truck, and then he reappeared lugging two sleeping bags under one arm and a huge picnic basket under the other. From inside the basket he withdrew a shiny red apple and handed it to Katherine. "Here, eat this while I set up our dinner."

She bit into the apple eagerly and watched as Joe prepared their indoor picnic. He unzipped the sleeping bags and spread them out in front of the hearth. When they were neat and smooth as a tablecloth, he began taking a variety of fresh fruit and cheeses out of the basket, along with plates, silverware, napkins, and glasses. He hadn't forgotten a thing. Last of all, out came a bottle of red wine and a corkscrew. When the "table" was set, he crossed over to a stack of logs and kindling and started to build a fire in the fireplace.

As he hunkered over the task, Katherine reached out and ran her fingers along the strong line of his jaw. "Do you always carry a picnic basket in your truck, just in case you come upon a hungry female?"

"I thought it would be nice to have our dinner here and watch the sunset together."

Katherine felt as though her insides had begun to melt. In the past few days she'd thought of Joe in many ways—handsome, masculine, strong, exciting—but never as romantic.

When the fire was going well, Joe removed his jacket and Katherine did the same. The ingestion of one little apple had not totally cured her queasy stomach, but she did feel a bit better as she moved to sit beside him on the floor.

Outside, as promised, the sun had begun to set and above the towering Douglas firs and ponderosa pines they saw a sky alight with a wash of brilliant dusk colors that reflected upon the surface of the calm lake waters.

They started dinner in a cross-legged sitting position that soon gave way to lying on their sides supported by a bent elbow and then finally to reclining fully, side by side on their stomachs, chins resting on folded hands.

While Joe poured her another glass of wine, Katherine was acutely, expectantly aware of the contact of shoulder, hip, and leg as he lay beside her. "The sunset's all gone," she declared, "but I think I like the dark even better. Why is it that a mountain sky seems brighter and more star-filled than the nights down below?"

"People down there say it's because their sky is cluttered up with the lights from millions of houses and buildings and that it only *seems* our nights are clearer because we're sparsely populated and the mountain goes all black at night." Joe slipped his arm around Katherine's waist and nuzzled her neck playfully. "But I don't believe that for a second, do you?"

He set down his glass and then took Katherine's out of her hand. Rolling over on his back, Joe pulled her with him so that she was pressed along the length of his body. He reached up to smooth back the pale blond hair that fell across her face. "I think our dark mountain skylines are made special for nights like this," he whispered urgently, his mouth tracing butterfly kisses over her mouth.

Katherine sighed as a longing heat flamed deep inside her. A deep purring sound, mingled with a moan, rose up hungrily from her throat. Katherine's mouth parted slowly, opening itself to Joe's demanding tongue. The tip of it lightly, teasingly touched her own, and she gasped softly, as though a jolt of electricity had passed through her entire body, and she clung to him as a surge of desire and need threatened to steal away her senses.

But there was still one rather embarrassing detail to attend before giving in completely to the moment. "I don't know about you, Joe"—she smiled weakly—"but I've got two layers of clothes on under this sweater and I can't think of a single way of getting out of them gracefully."

Joe threw back his head and laughed. "Woman, you really know how to squeeze the romance out of a carefully planned seduction. I'd have thought of something, I promise. But as long as you've brought it up, okay, I'll admit the problem does tend to lessen some of the spontaneity. We'll just make do, all right?"

He sat up and started to unbutton his shirt. Meanwhile Katherine quickly pulled the sweater over her head, revealing a shirt and underneath that . . .

"What the hell. . . ?" Joe stared at the bright

red union suit Katherine wore as a last defense against the cold. "Where did you get *that* thing?"

Katherine took off her boots and unzipped her slacks, easing them down over her hips. The union suit was a one-piece woolen undergarment that covered her entire body from ankles and wrists to the base of her throat. Eight buttons fastened it together from crotch to neck.

"Well, let's see what you've got under that shirt and those jeans!" she demanded. "Ah-hah! Just as I thought. Gray long johns. Pretty boring stuff, Joe." She laughed as a shiver ran up her spine, and Joe lifted the end of one sleeping bag to drape over her shoulders.

The laughter died away slowly and they were left looking quietly into each other's eyes. Katherine's breath caught in her throat. She leaned forward and rested her cheek against his, content for the moment to relish the smooth warmth of his skin.

Then Joe's fingers began working the buttons beneath her neck, slowly, much too slowly, and when he had undone them to her waist he nudged the top of the undergarment off Katherine's shoulders and moved back slightly to look at her.

The light from the fire cast golden streaks across her flesh. Joe's hand wandered over her arm and cupped an exposed breast. He bent and teased it gently with his lips, feeling the nipple harden under his tongue. Katherine shuddered and stroked his lowered head, her fingers catching in the thick wavy mass of his hair. She moaned impatiently but his lips moved leisurely to explore the soft curve of her neck and then his teeth nipped gently at the lobe of her ear.

Katherine's hands reached behind his back, and with an anxious tug brought the gray undershirt up over his head. He pulled her into his lap and held her there, her breasts pressed to his bare chest, touching and caressing until there wasn't a valley or plain that had not been sought out and lovingly praised.

Joe's lips traced a fevered path to Katherine's soft, trembling mouth and his kiss became more demanding. Her whole body quivered in response. She was only vaguely aware that somewhere between the first touch of Joe's hands and this moment, they had both been divested of every last stitch of clothing. Some small part of her warned Katherine that she was in danger of becoming too deeply involved, that the feelings he so easily roused within her might become a habit she wouldn't have the strength to break, but the warning came too late. She was tensed to the point of screaming for release, trembling uncontrollably as Joe's mouth moved slowly over her throat, her breasts, along the silken curves of her cheeks. He pulled her even closer, but it still wasn't enough. She wanted more, tightening her arms around his neck, straining to feel his flesh against hers, glorying in the telltale throbbing of his body under her thigh.

He groaned heavily and pushed her back into the softness of the down-filled sleeping bag, pausing only long enough to draw the other one over his back as he covered Katherine with the heat of his lean, hard body. His fingers set her flesh on fire, tracing an insistent, searching line over her hips and between the moist heat of her legs. She could feel him there, waiting, teasing, parting that eager spot with an agonizing and delicious anticipation. And then he was moving slowly upon her, inside her, and she clung to him, swaying in his rhythm, her back arched invitingly, awash in a sea of exploding sensation and light, lost to the pleasure of giving and receiving the gift of consummate passion.

Chapter Four

The sound of the truck's ignition turning over corresponded precisely with the uncontrollable shiver that raced up Katherine's back and settled into her quaking shoulders. While the engine idled and warmed, Joe looked over at her and placed his right hand on Katherine's leg, hooking his fingers between her thighs and edging her across the seat until she was pressed alongside him. The front of her jacket was unbuttoned and now his arm rested against her chest, his hand still tucked tightly between her legs. The touch seemed to Katherine very personal and highly erotic, as though Joe was reluctant to sever the invisible bond that joined them. The intimacy left her shaken and wordless. And comfortable. She wanted nothing more than to sit back quietly and relive every moment of their evening together, to savor the excitement of being with him, the touch and feel of him. It was still too soon for words, and Joe seemed to share her appreciation of the silence. Katherine thought nothing ruined the afterglow more than a partner who immediately launched into a clinical dialogue on his response to stimuli. She was gratified to learn that Joe was more of a doer than a talker.

Using only his left hand, Joe guided the Blazer out of the driveway and onto the highway. Katherine rested her head on his shoulder and closed her eyes, lulled by the aftermath of lovemaking and the hum of the truck as it sped over the road. She was so relaxed she felt like wax melting against the heat of him.

How long had it been since she had felt such a marvelous sense of contentment and fulfillment? After the prolonged affair with Chris Massey there had been a few false starts with other men, brief couplings that had left her dissatisfied and anxious to pull away. If she was going to be totally honest with herself, Katherine had to admit that even sex with Chris had been more fulfilling physically than emotionally.

So what it all came down to was this: Katherine was thirty-two years old, she had been with famous and powerful men in some of the most romantic settings imaginable, and no one had ever made her feel as gloriously sensual and quietly peaceful as this hometown boy had managed to do.

Be careful what you wish for, Katherine's daddy had been fond of saying; you just might get it. The words had never seemed more poignant than at this moment. Katherine had wanted a casual affair with Joe, and now that it had begun, she was suddenly afraid that "casual" was not going to be enough for her. Just how much more she wanted, she was not yet completely sure about.

But at that precise moment she wondered if "everything" was a bit excessive.

"First snow," Joe murmured softly, almost to himself. The arm that rested against Katherine's breast moved away briefly as he turned on the windshield wipers.

Katherine opened her eyes and stared straight ahead. The delicate flakes drifted down on the windshield for only a second before being pushed off to the sides.

If the fall kept up, she would awaken to a snow-laden village in the morning. Even the landscape would be fresh and new tomorrow. Her fingers caressed Joe's hand unconsciously and she nuzzled her cheek against his shoulder.

"Can we stop and get out?" She laughed at the lunacy of her sudden request, offering a light shrug. "Just for a minute?"

Joe grinned and shook his head as though he didn't quite take her seriously. "You're not dressed for it. Are you sure you want to wander around in a snowfall in near-freezing weather at this ungodly hour?"

"Are you kidding?" Katherine frowned playfully as she tucked her hair into the tweed cap and began buttoning her jacket. "You're talking to a woman who takes long walks in blinding rain in her bare feet!" She laughed again. "I like to feel the mud and water squish between my toes."

Joe turned into the parking lot of Rim High School and shut off the engine before giving Katherine one of his sternest professional frowns. "As your doctor, I don't recommend this. But I'll go along with it as long as you promise to keep your shoes where they belong.''

Katherine smiled and raised a hand in pledge, starting slightly when Joe bent to kiss her softly on the lips. For just a split second, a heartbeat, she saw on his face an expression she was unable to identify. Then it was gone and Joe stepped out of the cab, offering a hand to help Katherine down.

The parking lot of the high school was illuminated by two overhead lights, both of which were almost totally obliterated by the heavy snowfall. The school itself was in darkness, a somber gray concrete structure that made up in sturdiness and practicality what it lacked in beauty. Joe left her only long enough to get a flashlight out of the back of the Blazer, and when he returned, one arm went around Katherine's shoulders in a protective gesture that made her stomach turn over in a flutter.

Heads down against the direct fall of the snow, they raced to the front entrance of the school and stood for a moment brushing the wet snow off their clothes. Joe spun Katherine around and swiped at the moisture on her jacket and the seat of her pants, pausing a moment to cup the sweetly rounded curve in his hand before leading her off past the administration office and toward the arts wing of the school.

The hazy glow of the flashlight did little more than pierce the dense snowfall and cast a pale, eerie light on the concrete walls of the building. Beyond a few feet, their visibility was almost nil. Katherine had never been one to imagine huge lurking things in the darkness. She was more concerned with tripping over a ledge than with running into an unfriendly presence, at least here in Rimforest. Strange, but it hadn't occurred to her until just this moment that she felt safe—in body and in mind—for the first time in years.

Each room they passed brought on a rush of "do you remember?" and "did you ever?" During high school, beyond the three R's, Katherine and Joe had pursued different interests and so had shared very few classes together. Now those differences made for lively and funny vignettes. Katherine was astonished to learn who it was that had left stinkbombs made of magnesium and sulfur on the table in the teachers' lounge every Friday afternoon. As for the graffiti in the boys' bathroom, Joe only said it was randy enough to be whitewashed with prudent regularity. Those antics all sounded pretty childish now, but in the "good ole days" foul-smelling messages to the teachers and dirty limmericks were good for a chuckle.

The hasty tour ended at the gym. Katherine put her hand on the cold steel bar across its double doors and sighed. "The last time I saw this place it was being decorated with colored streamers and tissue-paper clouds. 'A Night of Heaven'—wasn't that the theme of our senior prom?"

Joe's arm slipped and dropped away from her shoulders. "I don't remember," he muttered shortly, darkly. "Let's get back to the truck, shall we?"

Katherine stepped between Joe and the stairs leading out. "Wait a minute," she demanded incredulously. "You're not still holding a grudge, are you?" Joe's silence was answer enough. "I can't believe it! Joe, that was fifteen years ago. We were kids. Come on, you're not going to stand there and tell me—"

"I'm not telling you anything," Joe broke in impatiently. "You're right. It *was* a long time ago. Forget it. Look"—he started to move past her—"I've got office hours early tomorrow morning and it's getting late. I'd better get you home."

"No," Katherine replied stubbornly. "If this is going to be a problem, let's deal with it. Now."

Joe sighed heavily and shifted from one foot to the other. "It's not a problem, okay? Something more important came up and you couldn't make it." He shrugged. "Simple enough."

"I tried to call you," Katherine protested, a little exasperated. "To explain, but you weren't anywhere around and there was no answer at your folks' house."

Joe scowled. "I was in San Bernardino picking up my tux and your corsage that morning, but I was home in the afternoon. Maybe you should have tried harder."

"Yeah, okay." Katherine squared her shoulders. "And maybe you should have mentioned this leftover resentment before we traipsed off to your house for a candlelit picnic and parlor games. What were you doing tonight, Joe?" Her voice caught suddenly. "Exorcising a few old demons? Getting even with the seventeen-year-old girl who stood you up fifteen damn years ago?"

To her surprise, Joe began to laugh softly. He reached out and pulled Katherine's stiff, resisting body into the shelter of his arms, whispering against her cheek. "Hey, what are *you* getting so fired up about? I was the one all dressed up and no place to go, remember?" He backed off a little and squinted at her through the darkness. "I don't know why it still bothers me. I suppose because it was you. If it had been someone else I probably would have forgotten it long ago, but"— he grinned sheepishly, and if it hadn't been so dark, Katherine might have seen him color uncomfortably—"it was always *you* when we were kids. I was crazy about you, even then. You women seem to think you've got the market cornered when it comes to sentiment and tender feelings. That silly dance meant a lot to me, my big chance to impress you and win your heart forever." He smiled at the corny line he'd just used and then sobered again. "God, I can still remember how it felt when I drove over to pick you up and the house was so dark and silent."

"Did you hate me then?" Katherine's arms slipped around Joe's waist.

"Yes," he answered simply. "And for a long time after that, too."

Katherine tensed. "And now?"

Joe's mouth lowered to brush across her cheek. "Now I'm crazy about you all over again."

The porch of Katherine's cabin was bathed in shimmering streaks of moonlight and dark shadows. She moved silently into the circle of Joe's arms and sighed as she felt his embrace tighten around her. Katherine returned the gesture happily, her fingers brushing lightly along the back seam of Joe's heavy winter jacket. There were so many things she wanted to tell him, so many things she longed to share with him. But foremost in her mind was the thought of how much the closeness they had shared meant to her, how grateful she was to have discovered, at just this precise moment in her life, the simple joy of falling in love with him all over again.

"If I could bottle the way I feel tonight," Katherine murmured against the cool flesh of his neck, "I'd pour myself a dose of Joe at the start of every day." She kissed the spot her lips had touched and smiled. "Mercer's Magic Elixir. That and a two-week vacation, guaranteed to cure what ails you."

She was uncomfortable with the words the moment they were spoken. She sounded as though she wanted no more from Joe than what could be squeezed in between now and the time she was scheduled to return to Los Angeles. Her choice of words must have hit Joe much the same way, because his chuckling response had a stilted, forced ring to it and Katherine felt his arms drop slowly from around her waist.

"I'm a doctor." His normally husky voice took on a light, calculated tone. "It's my job to prescribe the proper medicine. Although," he added with a shrug, "I don't make any guarantees without the usual six-week follow-up."

"Take all the time you need, Joe." Katherine's arms slipped around his neck to reestablish the contact between them. "I'm in no hurry." She was nearly overcome by the feeling that, short of a good long talk, nothing was going to help smooth over the damage that one thoughtless statement had made. He was trying to act as if he wasn't bothered, but Katherine clearly sensed he was upset. If she had learned anything about Joe in the past few days, it was that nothing had the effect of putting him on the defensive quicker than she did. His professional ethics might be questioned, his new house might be likened to a shack, and he would scowl slightly, arch a brow, and tell the offender to buzz off. Only she had the power to raise his hackles and start his teeth to grinding.

This was neither the time nor the place to enter into a discussion of what they expected from each other. Katherine was not yet sure just how much she wanted, and she had never been one to play phony romantic games. She neither made empty promises nor started anything she was not prepared to follow through on. When Joe knew her better, she hoped it was a trait he would come to admire in her, but for now, all that would have to wait until she wasn't so exhausted and confused.

Katherine dug through the contents of her purse, searching for the cabin key. "Will I see you tomorrow?"

"I don't know." Joe cleared his throat self-consciously. "I'll have to call you on it, but Wednesday is bad for me because I have an appointment at the house with the guy who'll be pouring the concrete for the driveway. And"—he started backing away as he spoke—"Thursday and Friday nights I'm pulling duty at the hospital.

The way it looks now, I won't have any free time until the reunion Saturday night."

Joe was so obviously groping for any excuse to avoid seeing her that Katherine was stunned into silence. Was this the same man who only twenty minutes earlier had said he was still crazy about her? Well, Katherine was still flushed with just those same feelings, but not so light-headed as to toss aside her pride completely. She certainly wasn't going to beg him.

She turned away to open the cabin door. "Whatever." She shrugged lightly and stood on tiptoe to place a quick kiss on Joe's cheek. Still, she had more trouble than she wanted to admit keeping the tremor from her voice as she added, "Just give me a call and leave a message with Molly if I'm not in."

When she had closed the door behind her, Katherine listened for the sound of Joe's footsteps as he left the porch. It was a few minutes before she finally heard them, almost as though he had been standing there wondering—as she was—how something that had begun so beautifully had skidded to an abrupt, painful halt. Katherine crossed the darkened room and turned on the light beside her bed. She sat down heavily, feeling as though someone had punched her in the stomach and she had lost all her breath in one long gasp.

What the hell had happened out there on the porch? One little comment, an unfortunate choice of words, and she could actually see him begin to shy away from her.

All right. Maybe it wasn't the best moment to remind them both that she was only in Rimforest for a two-week vacation. But she hadn't meant to sound as if at the stroke of midnight on the fourteenth day she intended to vanish in a cloud of perfume-scented smoke, never to be seen again.

And Joe had no reason to take her words—a compliment, really—so literally.

It had been wonderful between them. Katherine would not even attempt to deny that. But why did Joe have to make it more than it was? They were two adults, after all, undeniably drawn to each other and free to explore their mutual attraction. Katherine vibrated like a pressure cooker with the good feelings that were still building inside of her. And, up to a few minutes ago, she would have bet an arm that Joe felt exactly the same way. Now it seemed he wanted more. A declaration of some kind. A—the thought of it made her mouth go dry—commitment.

Katherine got to her feet again and began to struggle out of her damp jacket. She shivered and hurried over to the fireplace to start a warming fire. For at least ten minutes her thoughts were focused on the task, but as soon as the heat started to penetrate her numbed hands, she found herself thinking of Joe again.

He's probably at home right now, thinking about how childishly he acted and wishing I had a telephone so he could call and apologize. Katherine smiled and rubbed her hands together over the heat of the fire. Joe would see that he'd overreacted and be embarrassed by the way he'd behaved. If Katherine had sidled up to him and whispered, "Hey, sailor, want to buy a working girl a drink?" Joe couldn't have been more of-

fended or put off. He was wearing her Aunt
Minnie's face when he started backing away from
her. Tight, prudish. Positively stung!

A thought suddenly occurred to Katherine and
she rechecked the fire before scrambling off to
the bathroom. If she was going to be rested in the
morning when Joe stopped by, she had better get
to bed and stop all this unnecessary reflection on
a silly incident that would resolve itself when
Joe thought better of it. He didn't really intend
to let four days pass without seeing her. Did he?

Somehow, Katherine had expected the place to
be decorated in streamers and balloons, with a
big bowl of thoroughly awful watered-down punch
and a plate of "chicken surprise" as the main
entrée. Instead, someone had gone to the trouble
of gathering fresh evergreen boughs and fashion-
ing them into centerpieces that sat atop white
linen tablecloths. A full bar was set up in a small
room adjoining the dining area, and the only
concession to the fact that this was a reunion
instead of a large corporate banquet was a banner reading "Welcome Back Rim High School
Alumni" that hovered over the heads of a five-
piece band just beginning to set up as the dinner
dishes were cleared away.

Katherine's *boeuf en daube* sat untouched on
the plate in front of her and she barely noticed
when the waiter hesitated before taking it from
the table. It was all she could do to keep a slight
smile pasted to her lips and pretend to be listening to the conversation around her while scan-
ning the faces of late arrivals. There was a delicate

balance to be reached here. Katherine wanted to see Joe *before* he noticed her so that she would not be taken by surprise, but, more important, she did not want to be caught anxiously swiveling her head from one end of the room to the other like a spectator watching a fierce tennis competition.

On the morning after what Katherine had considered an unimportant tiff, she'd waited expectantly for a call from Joe, loitering outside the office of the Retreat, feigning an almost obsessive interest in the local flora and fauna. Molly Flynn must have thought she was playing without a full deck. On the second day, Katherine told herself, "I am not a sixteen-year-old girl whose whole life hinges on the sound of a telephone ringing." She had forced herself to climb behind the wheel of her car, *after* leaving a full itinerary of where she could be reached if the need arose. Which it didn't. By the third day, she was steaming. But on the morning of the fourth day, Katherine arose with an icy calm, wondering if her agent, Larry Michaels, knew the name and number of a first-rate hit man. She soon discarded the notion as excessive and set about concentrating on the only behavior pattern with which she felt comfortable. And after having portrayed Leanne Cameron for close to fifteen years, Katherine was confident of success.

She was, as they say, dressed to kill. She had never looked better in her life and she knew it. A quick trip up the mountain to one of Big Bear Lake's overpriced but fashionable dress shops had remedied the "nothing-to-wear" blues. All the makeup Katherine had hidden away that first night came back out of the kit and she spent three hours before Janet and Andy came to pick her up fixing her hair and nails and masterfully blending several shades of eye shadow and two tones of blusher with a final dusting of gold-brilliant highlight for good measure.

Now Katherine sat with an outward appearance of serenity at the oval table she shared with the Sheas. The golden-brown silk dress she wore was clingy, fitting the smooth curves of her body like a second skin. The neckline draped over the swell of her breasts and she wore no jewelry to distract a man's eyes from the sight of the gentle rise and fall of her chest. Katherine's pale hair was blown dry and hot-curled into a study of casual disarray, the sides full and swept back to reveal the small lobes of her ears, decorated by simple gold studs that shimmered with every turn of her head.

She was ready for him now, armed with just the right combination of staggering beauty and an attitude of studied condescension. All she needed was the target of her animosity. But with each passing minute, Katherine's spirits flagged.

He wasn't going to show up. She had gone to all this painstaking time and effort to appear the untouchable glamour girl and Joe wasn't even going to have the decency to show up and be amazed by it. And to be sorry for it. Sorry that he had expected too much, wanted more than Katherine was ready to offer. Repentant that he had not just seized the moment and enjoyed it, as Katherine had intended to do.

But no. It wasn't in Joe Mercer's character to have the simple courtesy to allow Katherine her moment of carefully planned reprisal. Coward!

"What did you say?" Janet Shea blinked in surprise and leaned closer.

"What?" Katherine's eyes widened innocently as she felt a glowing flush start to spread.

"You've been sitting there like a sphinx all evening, Katie," Janet admonished with a grin. "The only sound I've heard out of you is the faint grinding of your teeth. What's wrong with you?"

"Nothing." Katherine laughed weakly, brushing aside Janet's query. "I'm just winding down, I guess. A little like the letdown after Christmas or postpartum blues."

"Winding down?" Janet repeated, shaking her dark head. "Katie, it's only nine o'clock. The night is still young, my girl. You better snap out of it or you'll be comatose by eleven. I know exactly what's on the agenda for tonight and I can promise you won't be ready for bed until the wee hours."

"My God," Katherine countered, relaxing a little. "Sounds ominous. Maybe you better fill me in."

"Well . . ." Janet's hand fiddled with the lace collar of her maternity dress in a gesture of comic eagerness to gossip. "After all this mess is cleared away, we have until ten to mingle and hit the bar like a hoard of thirsty buffalo. At precisely ten o'clock, Susie Shoemaker, as coordinator of this epic event, will take her place behind the microphone and launch into a speech she's been re-

hearsing for months. I've had to play audience
several times, but the speech is really kind of
cute and she plans to give out awards to the
person who traveled the farthest to be here, the
one with the most children, that kind of thing.
Then we dance until midnight, at which time
horse-drawn wagons pull up in front and we all
pile on for a hayride guaranteed to put the bloom
back in your cheeks. Our destination will be—Oh,
hi, Joe. It's about time you got here."

"Joe." Katherine nodded shortly and shifted
back into her original position. Her look was brief
but more than long enough to take in the sight of
him dressed in an immaculate dark-gray blazer.
His shirt was a muted rose color, his tie slightly
darker, and the cashmere sweater he wore under
his jacket was a shade off white.

Damn him, Katherine thought as her stomach
turned over. She was a sucker for a man in a
sweater. Always had been. Why couldn't he have
shown up in a slightly outdated three-piece polyester suit? Something in a tacky shade of pale
blue that bagged at the knees and had the texture of tiny pebbles. Where did he get off with,
on top of everything else, having a sense of style?

Katherine managed to keep her expression pas-
sive and uninterested when Joe took the empty
seat beside her and began talking across the table
to Janet and Andy.

"Sorry, Jan, but babies have their own time-
tables. You'll find that out soon."

Janet, the unsuspecting traitor, beamed at Joe,
her hand going automatically to her rounded

stomach. Katherine could see the trust her friend had in Joe and it made her all the more irritable.

"Who was it?" Janet asked.

"Marjean Charles," Joe answered. "A boy. I want to talk to you, Katie." His hand closed over Katherine's shoulder in a gesture so abrupt she nearly jumped off the chair in surprise.

Katherine regained her composure instantly and pulled away with delicate and pointed disdain. "We have nothing to talk about," she hissed softly. "Go away."

"Stop acting like a brat." Joe made no attempt to keep his voice low. "It never has suited you. Look"—he raised both hands away from her—"I just want to talk about the other night, that's all. We can either do it in private or right here, but we *are* going to talk about it. I'm not going to float around all night with you shooting daggers at me from across the room. I've got something to say and I'm going to say it. Janet?" Joe smiled impishly. "You getting all this? Andy? How 'bout I give you a little background on the problem so you'll—"

"All right!" Katherine bristled angrily as she quickly got to her feet. "Excuse us a moment, will you?" The openmouthed surprise on the faces of everyone at the table brought a fresh surge of pink to her face. "This shouldn't take long." Katherine turned and kept her back stiff as she walked away from the table.

They stopped by the cloakroom to pick up Katherine's coat before going out to the abandoned patio. The tables and chairs were all covered with an inch layer of snow, so they stood huddled near the building under the protection of a sagging canopy.

"Well," Katherine demanded, pulling her coat close over her shoulders, "what is it that couldn't have waited another day? You've had no trouble putting off this little chat so far. Why now?"

Joe laughed shortly, without humor. "I couldn't take another day of this, especially since I knew I'd be in the same room with you all night."

"Well, you've waited too long to apologize." Katherine thrust out her chin defiantly. "I'm not interested anymore."

"I don't intend to apologize for anything," Joe countered calmly. "I took some time to think about what was starting between us and whether or not I could handle becoming involved with you. I'm a simple man, Katie. I can't begin to comprehend the ambitions and needs that keep you running on that treadmill in L.A. It's a fantasy to me, something that doesn't exist or have any substance in my life."

Katherine was hardly past the part where Joe had said he had nothing to be sorry for. What nerve! The man had the sensitivity of a gorilla! "Involved?" Katherine repeated haughtily. "A casual affair doesn't necessarily constitute life-long commitment, you know."

"Ah, Katie." Joe sighed and shook his head, moving closer so that she felt the wall of the building press against her back. "When are you going to admit that there has *never* been anything casual about the feelings we have for each other?" His mouth poised only inches from hers and she instinctively raised her face to him. "Not from the first time I pushed you into a mud puddle when you were six years old has there been anything but intense passion in the way you make me feel. No one has ever given me the highs and lows I get from you. It's scary, but I can't let it go now that you're back again."

"I may not be around for long." Katherine clutched desperately at her last defenses, her voice ringing strangled and breathless in her ears. There was not an ounce of anger left in her, but Katherine was still warily determined not to let the nearness of him and the feel of his breath warm upon her cheek sway her into making an impulsive, purely emotional commitment. "I won't promise how I'll feel about all this when it comes time for me to leave."

"I'll take my chances," Joe whispered softly. "I'm really quite a guy, you know. Loyal, charming, dedicated, even a little irresistible. A few more days with me and you'll sooner give up your Neilsen rating than walk away."

"Conceited, aren't you?" Katherine's hands went to Joe's chest, but she couldn't let them rest there. Her fingers snaked upward until she was clutching his shoulders and urging him closer.

"No," Joe breathed huskily before his mouth touched hers, "just determined."

Chapter Five

❧

Katherine stifled a yawn as she stood beside the sink in the cabin's tiny kitchen and put away the last of the dishes she'd used while preparing a light lunch. Janet Shea had not been exaggerating when she'd said the reunion celebration would take them into the wee hours. Thanks to a two-hour ride atop a wooden-planked wagon buffered by only a few strands of nearly frozen straw, Katherine's rear end felt like it had been blasted with two barrels of buckshot. And, with someone's insistence that they all follow up the hayride with a mass exodus down the mountain for breakfast at a twenty-four-hour restaurant, her aching body had collapsed into the soft warmth of her bed only minutes before the sun crept up over the trees.

Still, it was fun, even if Joe hadn't been there to enjoy it with her. At the stroke of midnight, his beeper sounded and he left the dance floor to use the phone, returning with a preoccupied frown and a brief explanation that he was needed back at the hospital. A real Cinderella, he was.

Think about what I said, he had whispered as he bent to kiss Katherine's cheek. And, damn

him, that was *all* she had been able to think of
since watching him leave the reunion. The rest
of the evening had passed pleasantly. After a few
congratulatory statements from old friends, Katherine had settled in to being Katie again, just as
her classmates all settled into being Will and
Connie and Susie again. Katherine's notoriety
vanished with the first recollection of how she
had rolled up her skirt at the waistline to shorten
it the moment she was a block from her house.

Even now the memory made her smile. Mother
had been strict. During the whole of Katherine's
tenth-grade year she had left the house a model
of fresh-scrubbed youth. One block later, out came
the pale shade of peach-colored lip gloss, her
skirt was rolled above her knees, and the sturdy
"good-for-your-feet" shoes were replaced by a
pair of scruffy white tennis shoes she kept at the
bottom of her book bag. The trick was remembering to put everything back the way it was when
school was over and she returned to the scrutiny
of her mother's gaze.

Katherine laughed aloud and turned away from
the sink, pausing to roll her head from side to
side in an effort to loosen the tightened muscles
that bunched between her shoulder blades.

Thank God she didn't do this often. A few
more nights of four and a half hours' sleep and
the faint circles under her eyes would begin to
look like she was carrying enough baggage to
circumnavigate the globe. The weary ache of her
thighs signaled a creeping atrophy. Her eyelids
were at half-mast.

I need a doctor, Katherine sighed inwardly.

She went into the bathroom to brush her teeth again before pulling a sweater over her head and reaching for her jacket.

It was a glorious afternoon, the ground ankle-deep in snow and the sun hovering bright and warm in a clear blue sky. Not a good sign for skiers, but terrific for anyone preferring a brisk walk and a cup of coffee on the porch, which was exactly what Katherine had in mind. A semi-jog to get the blood flowing, the heart pumping, and the cheeks glowing before paying a visit to Molly Flynn.

"Hello?" Katherine called out as the screen door slammed shut behind her. The ten-minute walk had done more than get her blood flowing. She was weak and winded. How, Katherine asked herself, does a woman who hasn't gained a pound since puberty get in such rotten shape?

"Well, hi there, Katie!" Molly thumped into the office. "Just having a quick lunch. What can I do for you?"

Katherine clucked apologetically. "No, I don't want to disturb you. Really, Molly, go back to your lunch. It's nothing important, truly, I was just looking to talk awhile. I'll come back later, okay?" She began to edge toward the door.

"Nonsense! Sit yourself down or, better yet, let's take a cup of coffee out on the porch and put our feet up for a while." Molly started bustling about, grabbing two cups, handing Katherine the pot before ushering her outside.

Once they were settled in the cushioned redwood chairs, Molly took a long sip and leveled her gaze upon Katherine. "There. Now, what's on your mind?"

The directness of Molly's question unsettled Katherine. She had planned to lead up to it slowly, to finesse Molly into spilling all she knew about Joe Mercer. Suddenly it didn't feel right and she coughed nervously, avoiding Molly's gaze. "I didn't have anything specific in mind. I suppose I just wanted some company." Katherine reddened even more as the lie rolled off her lips.

"Good!" Molly laughed heartily. "I wasn't in the mood for any 'deep' conversation anyway. It's too pretty out here to get all tied up with that. So, tell me, you enjoying your visit so far?"

"Ah, yes." She was thinking of Joe, and her answer was almost a sigh, but Katherine stopped herself quickly. "The reunion, you know. It was last night." She turned her face into the sun and squinted so that Molly's sharp eyes couldn't pick up the telltale blush that sprang up in Katherine's cheeks. "Funny, but hardly anyone seems to have changed much." Despite her own best instincts, Katherine started carefully tiptoeing around the true reason she had engaged Molly in conversation. "Of course, in high school I only knew a few people really well, so maybe I shouldn't make such a blanket statement. Janet Shea, for instance. Even in high school she wanted to be a wife and mother more than anything else, and now, here she is expecting the first of what she and Andy need to start their own baseball team. Do you know them, Molly? Now, Joe Mercer," Katherine went on after Molly's affirming but strangely silent nod, "I never would have figured him for a doctor. He was such a hell-raiser, we all thought he was destined to end up on the FBI's Most Wanted list.'' The chuckle her comment elicted from Molly was clearly a courtesy laugh, but Katherine was committed to her course of action now and she paused only a moment in the uncomfortable silence before hurrying on. "What do you think, Molly? Is Joe a really good doctor?"

"Yes," Molly answered without hesitation, "he's good. But Joe Mercer is more than just that. He walked out on a high-tone practice in the city and came home so that he could do what Doc Taley had taught him medicine was all about. You'll never see Joe Mercer sneaking a peek at his files to make sure he's got the first name of his patient right! He takes a personal interest in everybody in Rimforest."

"What about his ex-wife?" Katherine let it slip before she could stop herself, and then she had to concentrate on preventing herself from clapping a hand over her mouth in dismay at the clumsiness with which she had handled what was supposed to have been a subtle fact-finding talk. "He told me he was divorced," Katherine stammered, trying to redeem herself. "I just wondered if he ever brought his wife—"

"You'll have to ask Joe about that." Molly stood up, indicating she had nothing to say on the subject. "Look, honey, it's no secret you and Joe have been circling each other ever since you came back, but if you're really all that interested in some woman he hasn't seen in years, you better go to the source and stop wasting your time on this porch, because I've got too much respect for Joe Mercer to sit here and gossip about him."

Molly turned to leave and Katherine reached out quickly to put a hand on her arm. "I'm sorry, Molly," she said softly. "I guess I've lived in a glass house too long. I'd forgotten the privacy real people are entitled to enjoy."

"Well, that's all right, honey. It's forgotten already." Just as the warm smile returned to Molly's lips, the phone inside the office started ringing.

"It's for you, Katie," Molly poked her head out of the door and called. She smiled benevolently as Katherine hurried past, and then went out on the porch, leaving Katherine alone in the office to sample some of the privacy she had just mentioned.

"Joe?" Katherine didn't even bother saying hello. Her fingers curled gently around the receiver as though she could feel him through the telephone.

"Hey, beautiful . . ." He sounded tired and far away. "How you doing?"

"Fine. Where are you?"

"Home. Just now. My lady, Marjean Charles, had a bad time of it but she and the baby are okay now. I have to get some sleep. How 'bout dinner tonight?"

"Yes." Katherine smiled at the ease with which she said it. No games, no hesitation. "I'm going over to Green Valley with Janet and Andy, but I'll be back before six. Is that good for you?"

After they had said their good-byes, Katherine leaned against the desk and wondered how she was going to make it through the day. Fortunately the sound of a car pulling up into the snow-and-gravel-laden parking lot drew her attention and she looked oout to see the Sheas getting out of their car.

Good, Katherine mused lazily. I don't want one free minute to stop and really think about what I'm doing. This is the most fun I've had in years. Leanne Cameron feels a hundred miles away and I'm having the time of my life. Ah, Joe, just point me in the right direction and sweep me away.

She was late getting back from Green Valley and in a furor to shower and dress before Joe came by to get her. Katherine was just leaning over the bathroom sink, peering into the mirror with blusher in her hand, when a knock sounded at the door, twenty minutes early. She ran to answer it, her mouth dropping open at the features illuminated by the pale light on the porch.

"Aren't you Katherine Mallory?" Larry Michaels laughed heartily at the well-used joke and walked past her into the cabin.

Her theatrical agent was the last person Katherine had expected to see in Rimforest. "What are you doing here?" she demanded rudely, caught off-guard and more than a little annoyed. "You should have called first."

"Hello, Larry!" He mimicked a woman's voice. Undaunted, he answered with his own, "Hello, Katherine. It's great to see you. And I *did* call. All afternoon I called and some old bag refused to tell me where you were or when you'd be back or even if you were still alive."

"That was Molly." Katherine relaxed and shut the door, gesturing Larry toward the chair by the fireplace. "And she's not an old bag, my dear. She is a woman who believes in fiercely guarded privacy."

"Oh"—Larry grimaced comically—"one of *those!*" He paused to look around. "No wonder you're so grumpy. I told you to stay in Arrowhead. What a depressing dump! Can't you turn up the heat?"

Katherine laughed and pointed to the fire. "That *is* the heat. Get a little closer, it won't jump out at you. Really, Larry"—she frowned at the California-weight jacket he wore—"I told you it was real winter up here. You should have dressed warmer." Wet snowflakes clung to the thinning blond hair atop Larry's head. He was short and slim, as small-bodied as a boy. A tangle of gold chains hung damply at the neck of his polyester disco shirt. Larry Michaels might have looked the stereotype of a fast-talking, hustling Hollywood agent, but his large, pale blue eyes were sharp and keen and missed nothing.

"Yeah? Well, this place is still a dump," he grumbled as his fingers worked to untangle the chains around his neck. "I'd have been here earlier, but I had to stop at the bottom and buy snow tires, for Crissakes! Some jerk charged me fifty bucks, including installation. I bet he's still laughing and telling all his friends about the city slicker in the Rolls. Jerk!"

Strange, but Katherine had never noticed before just how hostile Larry could be. She was willing to bet the "jerk" was at least six feet tall. Larry took an instant dislike to anyone over five and a half feet.

"What was all the rush about?" Katherine checked the small Rolex on her wrist, wondering if Joe would be on time.

"Oh, baby," Larry said, brightening instantly. "Have I got a deal for you! I've got a meeting at ten tomorrow morning to pick up your new contract. It's a beauty, but of course I wanted to make sure you'd approve. Like I said, I called all afternoon and the barracuda at the desk wouldn't tell me a thing, so I decided to drive up. But let's get out of here. I can't talk a honey of a deal in this place. Does this burg have a restaurant with real napkins on the table or what?"

"Of course," Katherine snapped, making no effort to conceal her irritation. "But I'm not going anywhere. I have a date for dinner in fifteen minutes."

"A date?" Larry was dumbfounded. "A date? Forget the date, Katherine! I'm talking megabucks here, long-term contract, the works! Everything you said you wanted." His voice took on a stern, no-nonsense tone that reminded Katherine of her mother. "I've been working on this every day for a solid week, Katherine. The least you could do is pretend a little interest and let me take you someplace we can get a bottle of decent wine and toast our mutual success."

Katherine sighed inwardly. He was right, of course. She *did* owe him that courtesy. Larry Michaels had been her agent for over ten years—

fighting for her, protecting her. And now he had gone toe-to-toe with the studio in some very demanding negotiations and apparently emerged victorious. Katherine did owe Larry his moment of back-patting and congratulation. But that admission only served to make her wonder when she would have the freedom to owe *herself* something.

"Good idea." Katherine forced a big smile. "I'll finish getting ready and you warm up by the fire. Joe should be here in a few minutes. I'm sure he'll understand why I have to break our date," she whispered hopefully.

Katherine checked the time again and glanced over at Larry, watching as he fidgeted and all but fell asleep from feigned boredom. It was 6:17, two minutes later than the last time she checked. Joe had once mentioned that in his line of work punctuality was something attained only in his fantasies. Small-town doctors were notorious late arrivers and early departers. Last-minute calls from frantic parents, emergency house calls, being buttonholed on the way to his truck and asked for advice—it was all the natural order of things.

He was already twenty minutes late for their dinner date and there was no telling when he would finally arrive. For herself, Katherine would have waited patiently all evening, but Larry was making her crazy with those eyes raised to the heavens and the gaping yawns that cut through the uncomfortable silence of the cabin like a chain saw.

"Let's go." She scooped up her jacket and motioned to Larry. "I'll just stop by the office and tell Molly what's going on. She can tell Joe when he gets here."

"Five years, Katherine! Five years, and the figure I just quoted makes you the highest-paid actress on daytime television!" Larry sat back in his chair at the Rimview Inn and raised a wine-filled glass in Katherine's direction. "I knew you had the right stuff, kid. The studio is hot for you. I can't believe how much they're offering.

"What about vacations?" Katherine let the thought of an unheard-of five-year contract sink in. "I'm tired of having nothing but Leanne Cameron to look forward to. I need some rest."

"Rest?" Larry was genuinlly puzzled. "The time to rest is when the studio has the character of Leanne Cameron doling out advice about sex to young lovers instead of doing it herself."

"I don't know." Katherine sighed heavily and set her glass on the table. "Five years sounds like an eternity."

"Don't kid yourself, Katherine," Larry muttered brusquely. "You're a lucky woman. Most soap-opera characters take a fatal drive to Podunk after a few years. They're killed off or transferred out of state and the studio brings in fresh new characters to fill the void. You've had almost fifteen years, and now, another five guranteed. You should be thanking your guardian angel instead of hemming and hawing about vacations and all that other crap. You play your cards right and get a top-notch investment counselor and you'll be set for life."

"Sure"—Katherine frowned—"if I can stand my life by then." She had a vision of herself three years down the road, and it upset her more than the reaction she knew her answer was going to elicit from Larry Michaels. "No. No, I don't find the terms acceptable. I don't want to be trapped in a long-term contract."

"But that's not what we talked about last week," Larry sputtered indignantly. "You said—"

"I know what I said!" Katherine interrupted. "I said what my mother would have wanted me to say, what you wanted to hear. Well, not anymore. Lord, this feels good." Katherine grinned and felt the tension begin to drain out of her body. She sensed Larry wouldn't understand it— even Katherine was hard pressed to sort out the emotions she was experiencing—but at that moment, with everything she *thought* she wanted dangling out in front of her like a carrot before a stubborn mule, Katherine realized she wanted Joe even more. "Sorry, Larry, but I'm going to have to make more work for you. As far as *Bright Promise* goes, I'll tell you what I want and you tell the studio and maybe we can come to an agreement we all can live with." She reached over and patted Larry's hand. "I'm sorry you came all the way up here for nothing, Larry."

"Not for nothing, kiddo." He shook his head to clear it, shrugging lightly. "It's my job, the old 'kick-me, beat-me' syndrome. Agents take the flak from both sides. You've been a dream to work with—"

"Up until now?" Katherine suggested, smiling.

"—and I don't mind," he continued, "a little

discomfort for your sake. But I gotta tell you, Katherine, that's also my job. You're putting the kiss of death on a plum deal. I don't know how the network is going to take it." With that, he pulled out a dog-eared pad of paper and a pencil from the inside pocket of his jacket. "Okay, fire away."

Katherine hesitated, taking a deep breath. "I want a short-term contract, maybe just two or three years. Something that leaves me a great deal of time to do some living of my own. I'm tired of living vicariously through Leanne Cameron. She has all the fun and I take all the abuse" Katherine paused, assembling her thoughts so that she wouldn't forget anything. "I want the freedom to do other roles. And time off, away from the studio." She smiled slightly, secretly. "That's the most important thing. It's past the time I should have taken something for myself. Oh, before I forget . . ." Katherine continued speaking as new ideas sprang into her mind. Once started, she talked for twenty minutes.

When she was finished dictating the terms of a counteroffer she felt she could live with, a rush of contentment settled over her and she leaned back, eyeing Larry with a smile. "Well, what do you think?"

He shuddered. "I think this mountain air has made you crazy."

"What are you going to do?"

"What I'm gonna do is this: tomorrow morning I'm going to keep my appointment and lay this all out and then I'm going to take cover under a desk. That's what I'm gonna do."

"Really?" Katherine laughed softly. "You think it's really all that bad? Too prima-donna?"

"What *I* think doesn't matter. It's what four studio big shots and their team of lawyers think that counts. Come on, kiddo." Larry reached for the check. "I'll take you back to that rustic hellhole and then I've got to beat a path back to L.A. There must be some way to word all this so it doesn't read like a passage from *The Greta Garbo Guidebook to Life*."

Chapter Six

❧

Last night the switchboard operator at Joe's answering service had told Katherine that Dr. Mercer was not on call. He was out and the best the operator could do was to transfer Katherine's call to a Dr. Wegner. It didn't matter that Katherine told the woman her call was personal and to please ring through Joe's home. The answer came back the same, as though the operator had an eternal taped message lodged in her throat. The doctor is out, he is not on call, Dr. Wegner is taking Dr. Mercer's calls this evening.

Not this one, he isn't! Katherine had replaced the receiver in its cradle. Before bidding Molly a final good night, she made a mental note to change her own answering service. Someone was always coming up with a reason *her* service thought good enough for them to ring through to Katherine. But not Joe's! He was as guarded as the gold at Fort Knox. Unless, of course, he had specifically instructed that any and all calls from Katherine Mallory be turned away.

No, Katherine had told herself as she trudged back through the dark to her cabin. What a silly, paranoid thought.

Now it was morning, and in a few more minutes Joe's office would be open to patients. Katherine dialed the number and got the answering service which informed her that the office opened at nine o'clock and that unless it was an emergency she would have to call back. She waited until the second hand on the old school clock hanging in Molly's office swept past the twelve and began dialing again. The nurse in Joe's office told her the doctor was in with a patient and became quite cool in her manner when Katherine suggested that perhaps she could hold the line and catch him as he went from one examining room to another.

After leaving her name and number with a message for Joe to call her during the office lunch break, Katherine used every ounce of her control to keep from throwing the telephone across the room.

"Why do you suppose," she asked Molly through clenched teeth, "the nurses in *all* doctors' offices do everything they can to keep actual contact with the doctor at a minimum?"

Molly's face crinkled behind her rimless glasses. "Why, that's what they're there for, isn't it? A kind of buffer to weed out the hypochondriacs and layabouts from the sick people." She laughed and set aside the needlepoint she was working on. "Besides, Pam has always been pretty fierce about Joe's time."

"Pam?" Katherine's mouth quivered. "Pam Jaimet is Joe's nurse?"

"Not a full-fledged nurse." Molly grinned wickedly, deliberately ignoring the true meaning

behind Katherine's astonishment. "I think she's
an LVN—Licensed Vocational Nurse. Been working with Joe for a little over a year now. She does
her job real good, judging by the success you just
had trying to reach him."

"His nurse," Katherine muttered to herself,
"eight hours a day, all week long! Why didn't he
tell me?"

"Probably knew how you'd react," Molly replied sensibly. Then she sobered and walked over
to Katherine, putting an arm around her shoulders.
"Look, honey, you've been going about this whole
thing like your life was a soap opera. You're
acting like somebody else is writing this for you,
telling you what to say, directing all your moves.
Like last night—you wanted to keep your dinner
date with Joe but you let that pushy little squirt
call all the shots. And now you're working yourself up into a lather because Joe didn't tell you
Pam worked for him." Molly tsk'd impatiently,
giving Katherine a quick hug. "Well, so what?
It's you that's got him howling at the moon. Poor
Pam's been trying for years, and the closest she's
got is behind the desk in his waiting room. Tell
me something, Katie, if this was one of your
sudsy scripts, what would be your next move?
You'd make sure to run into him someplace, right?
And you'd shoot him a look to cut him off at the
knees and give him a big brush-off, right?" Despite herself, Katherine had to respond with a
smile. "Then," Molly continued, "you'd go on
back to your quiet, lonely cabin and congratulate
yourself for getting in the last dig. *And* you'd
spend another night by yourself. Now, *that's* what

I call real life!" Molly shook her head in disgust. "Why don't you think about it a bit and decide what *you* want to do, not what some half-baked pen pusher would write for you. Get yourself busy, girl! Don't mope around. I'll let you know when Joe calls." Molly pulled Katherine toward the door. "Now, buzz off. I've got work to do!"

With that and a quick hug, Molly turned away, but not before Katherine had placed a quick kiss atop her head.

"Thanks, Molly," Katherine sighed as the older woman hobbled back to the desk. "I think I'll go for a drive. So long." She closed the door quietly behind her and stood on the porch for a moment, deciding what exactly she felt like doing.

Janet and Andy had been wonderful but she was tired of looking through one cabin after another in her search for the perfect place. Janet, of course, would be at the office already, so it was doubtful that she was free to go out on anything other than business. Katherine's old school friends were, for the most part, being put up at the Arrowhead Inn and she supposed she could go there and hang around in the lobby until some one came down for a late breakfast. Or she might go up to Big Bear and rent a pair of skis, hit the slopes again after all these years.

But what she really wanted to do was be alone. Not alone in the true sense of the word, off in a cave with nothing but silence and eternity surrounding her. No, what Katherine wanted to do was go window-shopping, to stroll past shops and finger all the merchandise. That kind of slightly distracted solitude appealed to her at the moment.

The Arrowhead Village was perfect for her needs, Katherine decided as she made a quick stop at her cabin to collect a jacket and her purse. It was only fifteen minutes away and had an open mall built at the shoreline of Lake Arrowhead, loaded with small shops lining a wide, picturesque promenade. If worse came to worst she could sit and watch the tourists' children at the bumper boat ramp. A perfect, quiet, lazy kind of day.

As it turned out, several of Rim High School's alumni had exactly the same idea. Katherine no sooner pulled into the parking lot at the village than she heard her name called and it was hours before she could gracefully extract herself. When she got back to the Retreat, Molly told her the only call that had come in for her was one from Larry Michaels. Katherine returned it immediately, not anxious to risk another surprise visit, and was informed that her agent had submitted the new terms to the studio and was waiting for a callback.

When the door to her cabin closed behind her, Katherine knew precisely what she wanted to do next. It was nearly three in the afternoon; another hour and Joe's office would be closed for the day. And if she had to lurk behind a bush and spring at him as he walked down the steps, she was going to talk to him. She was going to shower now and put on fresh clothes and the most seductive perfume in her arsenal and then she was going to drive over to his office and lie in wait.

She pulled some clothes from the tall oak wardrobe chest—jeans, a lavender oxford shirt, a pale pink shetland sweater, soft leather boots—and spread them out on the bed before crossing over to the chest of drawers to take out the matching lace panties and bra she'd bought in Paris the year before on a location shooting for *Bright Promise.*

Katherine took her time. After the shower, as she dressed and put touches of spice-scented perfume behind her ears and at the pulse points of wrist, between her breasts, and behind her knees. She felt good, strong and sure of herself.

Joe *was* crazy about her. Every look and touch, the husky tone buried deep in his voice when he spoke to her, every instinct told her he was in love. And, better yet, Katherine wasn't thinking about anything except that, yes, she was in love, too. And it was the best, the most wonderful feeling of her entire life. To love and to be loved, to want to give herself wholly. To offer her heart over into someone else's keeping. Joe's keeping.

Joe. Even thinking his name was enough to send Katherine's pulse off and running. She loved the quiet strength of him, the sureness, the way he always seemed to know what was in her heart and mind, the way he had of making her feel peaceful and complete, content to live in her own skin.

A gray wool blazer complemented her outfit nicely but Katherine shivered as she went down

the path to her car. She hurried to rev up the
motor and start the heater going.

Joe's office was an old renovated two-story
wood-frame house. The front section facing the
street served as his office, and the back, entered
through an alley, as his living quarters. There
was parking along the street and Katherine pulled
neatly into a space, debating whether to wait in
her car or go into the office.

I might have to make an appointment, she
mused gaily. Better go in.

The door, when her hand closed around the
knob, was locked. A small handwritten note taped
at the corner of one of the door's glass panes
read, "Office closed at 3:00 today."

Je-e-ez, Katherine hissed, turning around in a
gesture of momentary helplessness. Well, she
asked herself archly, what now?

The front facade of the house was set up so
that a half-porch and shrubs blocked the side
access to the back of the building. The arrange-
ment was clearly an attempt to discourage anyone
going directly around back to knock on the doctor's
door. She would have to get back in her car,
drive down the street, and double back into the
alley and pull up on the opposite side of the
house.

Not on your tintype, fella. Katherine eyed the
shoulder-high shrubs warily. If Joe wasn't home,
it was best to leave her car out on the main drag
so that if he passed by, he would know she was
waiting for him in the back.

Katherine began making her way around the
side of the house, her feet sinking into the snow

up to her ankles. She moaned weakly. Three-hundred-dollar boots were getting water-stained, ruined! The shrubs loomed in front of her like a bushy white fence. They had grown together through the years until it was difficult to see where one began and another left off.

Katherine knelt and ran an ungloved hand from the ground up along the base of a shrub, parting it as she went and edging her way through the branches. Clumps of snow the size of Frisbees loosened and slipped from the shrubs, bouncing off her chest and legs as she ventured farther. Suddenly the shrub snapped shut behind her and she felt a wet and cold spray all over her face, clinging like tiny pearl beads in her hair. Nearly screaming with frustration, Katherine shouldered the rest of the way through to the other side. Then she stopped and worked furiously to brush the snow off her clothes and face, groaning as a small chunk slipped between her neck and the collar of her shirt.

She was irritated, and then, just as quickly, amused by the lunacy of the situation. If she had any doubts about being too much like Leanna Cameron, they vanished with a giggle. Leanne would have pointed a perfectly manicured finger, raised a perfectly shaped brow, and the shrubs would have been intimidated into parting like the Red Sea. Only Katherine Mallory would have gone lumbering around like a bad imitation of Laurel and Hardy.

She waded through the snow, heading toward the alley, and turned the corner. The entrance to Joe's bachelor apartment was a small three-tiered wooden step. Katherine pressed a cold finger to the buzzer and waited. No answer. The single parking stall to the left of the door was empty. Determined, Katherine kicked a thin layer of snow off the steps and sat down to wait, raising her face to the slight warmth of a quickly setting sun.

An hour later she was still waiting. The sun was down behind the trees and it was getting dark and colder by the minute. She might have gotten to her feet and walked around with her arms flapping to bring life back into her numbed limbs, except that she was afraid the seat of her pants was frozen to the steps and if she moved she would leave half her rear end behind.

The thought that she might never see another living soul, that they would find her huddled on Joe's doorstep like the poor little match girl, was only just becoming a real possibility when Katherine heard the sound of a powerful motor coming closer. The headlights, as Joe swung into his parking stall, swept across her face for a moment before coming to a stop against the window to her left.

"Katie?" he called as he got out of the Blazer and slammed the door shut. "What are you doing out here in the cold?" Joe bent to help her up and, surprisingly enough, she came away from the steps easily.

"Waiting for you," Katherine growled between chattering teeth. "What did you think?"

"Why didn't you just go in?" Joe's bland expression spoke volumes on just who had the least amount of common sense. "Door's open." His arm slipped around her hunched shoulders as he turned the knob, and led her in. "Heat's on, coffee's brewing. Get in there before you go into a state of hypothermia."

Once inside, Joe wrapped her in a blanket and started a blazing fire. He removed Katherine's boots and replaced them with a clean pair of his thermal socks.

"Let me help you out of your clothes." Joe made a move to reach inside the blanket to Katherine's soggy jacket.

"I'm *not*"—she jerked aside grandly—"in the mood for that, thank you very much."

"Right." Joe laughed and used his superior strength to force her body around again. "Neither am I," he assured her playfully. "Filthy, physical stuff." Shuddering in mock distaste, Joe set about pulling Katherine's arms out of the sleeves of her jacket. Still she resisted, more out of embarrassment than anything else. "Okay. You're a big girl and you'd rather do it yourself, right? Up stairs, in the loft, you'll find a sweater and a pair of sweatpants you can put on while your stuff dries."

Katherine nodded silently and trailed up the spiral stairs leading to Joe's bedroom, the blanket clasped around her shoulders dragging behind her. Ten minutes later she returned wearing a close-knit sailor sweater Joe had purchased at a surplus store and a pair of his gray drawsting sweats that hung on her slim hips like harem pants designed by Omar the tentmaker. So much for a carefully planned ensemble.

Joe took the pink sweater and lavender shirt,

the gray jacket and tight-fitting jeans from her hands, trading her a cup of coffee laced with brandy. He then left her for a minute while he spread the articles near the fire.

When he came back, he sank into an overstuffed chair and pulled Katherine gently into his lap. "Now," he said as his finger traced a tender path under her chin, "tell me why I found you camped on my doorstep instead of at your place, which is where I went right after my meeting with the salesman from the carpet place."

"You went by the Retreat?" Katherine concentrated on the hot liquid in her cup so that Joe couldn't see the intense relief that sprang into her eyes.

"Sure." He continued, "I had a three-thirty appointment so he could measure the yardage and give me an estimate, and then I drove over to see you. Why are you so surprised?"

Katherine sighed miserably. "I thought you were probably angry with me after last night. Why didn't you return my call this morning?"

"I didn't get a message to call you." He frowned slightly and brushed a strand of sandy-colored hair off his forehead.

"Then maybe you should have set Pam straight on just how much authority her job holds right from the first day you hired her." She said it casually but quite pointedly.

"Ah." Joe drew the sound out. "So you know. Look"—he raised his hands as though to ward Katherine off—"before you even ask it, the reason I never mentioned she worked for me is that I figured we had enough really important things to work out without being sidetracked by need-less jealousies. Besides, it's taken care of itself anyway. Pam gave me her two-week notice this morning. She's going up to Big Bear to work for Robert Lamb."

"Hm-m-m." Katherine snuggled closer to Joe and thought about that for a moment. "Is he married?"

"No." Joe mouth started moving against her neck. "I don't think so."

Satisfied, Katherine grinned smugly. "That figures." Then she started to giggle. "Pam Lamb. How perfectly awful!"

"She's a nice girl, Katie," Joe objected. "What'd she do to make you—"

"There's no such animal when two women are after the same man, my love," Katherine admon-ished him with a patient gaze.

"My God!" Joe's incredibly blue eyes flew open in mock terror. "Do you mean to say you're 'after' me?" His grip on Katherine eased immediately and he pretended to squirm in the chair. "Wait a minute. Just wait a minute! I was just counting on a brief affair, here, a couple of one-night stands, if you know what I mean. I never—"

"Oh, be quiet, you big oaf." Katherine's mouth curled into a pout. "And give us a kiss."

"No." Joe strained his neck to the side in an attempt to stay a few inches away from Kathe-rine's searching lips. "I won't be used and tossed aside like a comfortable old pair of bedroom slippers. If you want to get in my jeans again, lady, we'd better get a few things straight." His teasing resistance, begun in jest, ended on a serious note. But, once there, he floundered and hesitated before going on.

"Last night?" Katherine prompted softly, helpfully. "My agent, Larry Michaels, showed up unexpectedly with the terms the studio is offering on my new contract. I really didn't want to but I let him throw the old guilt-net over me and we went out to dinner to talk it over. I had a lousy time. Couldn't even concentrate for worrying about what you were thinking."

Joe flinched and slid farther down in the chair, taking Katherine with him. "You know, it's funny," he began softly. "I'm thirty-two years old, but when I walked up to that dark, silent cabin, I could have been seventeen all over again. Stood up on prom night. I went down to the office and talked to Molly, but it didn't really help the way I felt about it." He smiled to himself. "I guess men never fully lose the insecure lothario inside them."

"I'm sorry, Joe." Katherine's arms tightened around his neck, and she was suddenly aware of how her breasts were beginning to throb beneath the scratchy wool of Joe's borrowed sweater. "You have to remember . . ." She cleared her throat to rid it of its strained huskiness. "I've cared about only one thing in my whole life. My career. Everything else has revolved around that. It might take a little practice, a few clumsy starts and false stops, to get my priorities shifted around."

"I told you, Katie," Joe said as her hand caressed Katherine's arm, "I've got all the time you need." As his mouth hovered over hers, his tongue traced hot, moist circles over her lips.

Katherine gasped and parted her mouth, touching his tongue with her own.

"You've got the softest lips," Joe murmured deeply. "I like the way you kiss."

Katherine's eyes fluttered and closed. She sighed raggedly, straightening her legs and shifting her hips so that she reclined along the length of him. Joe eased her body into a comfortable niche between him and the arm of the chair, moaning in satisfaction when Katherine bent the knee of one leg and draped it over his hip. She was on fire for him, trembling, her chest surging erratically in an uneven, breathless rhythm. The rapid pounding of Joe's heart echoed against her breasts. His mouth clung to hers, demanding, relentless, consuming.

Katherine's hands slid over Joe's back, digging anxiously into the fabric of his shirt, momentarily frustrated in the effort to feel his flesh against her fluttering touch. She tugged the shirt loose at his waist and sighed ecstatically as her fingers reached their goal. He felt warm and smooth and strong.

Her excitement was heady, contagious. Joe shuddered, his response heightened by Katherine's eagerness. His hands grasped her hips and urged them closer to meet the slowly moving motion of his own. Katherine's arms moved upward and circled Joe's neck, clinging tightly. Now one hand trailed down along his chest, unbuttoning his shirt as it went. Katherine's mouth danced lightly down the length of his tautly corded neck, her tongue moving with the airless touch of a butterfly across his shoulder. Her fingers tucked gently

into the waistband of Joe's Levi's and in a quick
motion parted the zipper, and a sound—half growl,
half purr—erupted deep in his throat. Katherine
thrilled at the sound, opening her eyes to see
him watching her through half-veiled lids made
heavy with passion.

Wordlessly Katherine extracted herself from
Joe's embrace and got to her feet, standing shakily between his knees. She stretched and shook
slightly, trying for a semblance of control. A lop-
sided grin spread across her face. Her fingers
plucked at the drawstring of the sweatpants and
she rolled the heavy fabric down over her hips.
Then she delicately stepped out of the pants,
removing the thermal socks as well, standing before Joe in just his sweater and a lacy pair of
pale lavender bikini panties. In the time it had
taken her to discard the sweatpants, Joe had
removed his shoes and was now shrugging off his
shirt.

Katherine's heart fluttered and she swallowed
hard. Her hands trembled as she reached for the
bottom of the sweater and pulled it up over her
head. The only sound in the room was the crackling of the fire behind her and the sharp intake
of Joe's breath. He lifted his hips off the cushion
of the chair and began pulling off his jeans. Katherine bent to help, to hurry the task, and then
she shed the last piece of her own clothing.

Joe's hands reached up to grasp her waist, drawing her closer, guiding her. Katherine's knees
bent on either side of his hips, cushioned by the
padded fabric of the chair. She sighed longingly,

poised as she felt the hard maleness of him caress and enter her.

Joe's mouth moved over her shoulder, his teeth nipping gently at the soft flesh. the palms of his hands brushed across her breasts, fingertips stroking and enticing her nipples until Katherine thought she would scream. Her throat arched backward and a shudder ran the length of its delicate line.

Katherine's hips began moving in slow, small circles that gradually increased in tempo. Her fingertips clutched frantically at Joe's shoulders. She could feel him everywhere, touching her, engulfing her. I love you, Katherine promised silently. I love you, Joe.

Then there was no more time for thought. She was drowning in a raging sea of sensations. Bright, flashing, exploding sensations that captured and swept her away.

"You can come over here and ravish me anytime you want," Joe teased as he retied the drawstring tightly around Katherine's waist.

"Don't be tacky." Katherine batted playfully at his hands and then leaned against him, nuzzling her head under his chin. "Molly Flynn was right about you. You are an animal."

Joe laughed and lifted Katherine off her feet, hugging her fiercely. "I can think of a few more beastly things I'd like to do to you."

"I don't suppose feeding me is on that list, is it?"

"Right at the top," he assured her with a lascivious wink. "Have to keep your strength up, don't we?"

Katherine padded along behind him as Joe went into the kitchen and began rummaging around. It seemed to Katherine that he stood in the center of the narrow U-shaped kitchen with his arms outstretched, opening and shutting drawers and cabinets, clattering refrigerator and stove shelves. In less than ten minutes the steaks were under the broiler, a wild-rice concoction was simmering on the burner, and a Caesar salad sat on the counter ready to toss.

"So," Katherine muttered blandly, arching an eyebrow, "you can cook, too."

"Doesn't everyone?" Joe shrugged nonchalantly.

"I don't," Katherine admitted a bit sheepishly. "I never learned." She bristled at Joe's "you've-got-to-be-kidding" expression. "Look, I could if I wanted to, but I've never had the time. Before my mother died, she always took care of the house. And now, well, now I either eat out or I just throw on one of those frozen dinners. It's simpler that way. "

Joe said nothing, but his silence spoke volumes, as if he had a mental picture of Katherine sitting alone in her apartment, hunched over a metal tray filled with cardboard-flavored potatoes and soggy vegetables, planted in front of the television set for company. It wasn't a true vision—she usually had her meal on the run, standing over the counter in the kitchen—and she hastened to dispel the notion.

"I don't know why I should feel I have to justfy my eating habits," she groused impatiently.

"But I never have the time for gourmet cooking after filming at the studio, and on weekends I have my meals out." She frowned and added hastily, "With friends."

"Fine." Joe shrugged again, more than a little surprised and puzzled. "Why are you getting so defensive? *I* don't care whether you can cook or not. It's certainly not the basis of my attraction for you."

Katherine snickered softly and then decided to unload it all in one fell swoop. "The truth is, I'm not domestic at all. I can't cook or sew, and I have a cleaning lady in three times a week to do the housework." Her tone almost dared Joe to find fault with her life-style.

He chose not to. "Any more shattering confessions?" He smiled briefly at the shake of Katherine's head. "Good. Let's eat."

He handed her the salad to carry to the dining table while he transferred the rice into a serving bowl. Katherine came back for the plates and silverware, then sat down while Joe served.

It was all delicious. The rice dish had a well-blended nutty flavor, the salad was crisp and tangy, the steak perfectly medium-rare. Damn! One wilted lettuce leaf or a sticky piece of rice would have done wonders for her own self-esteem.

He's perfect, Katherine thought miserably. Perfect and noble and absolutely wonderful. He does everything well—from doctoring to cooking, from dancing to making love. He has the Midas touch. Everything he touches turns to perfect gold.

If I didn't love him so much, Katherine mused as she glanced over at him across the table, I'd hate him.

Chapter Seven

❧

Thursday was a good day, even if she did spend it without seeing Joe. His office was open later than usual, and directly after, he was scheduled to participate in a seminar at the medical school in Riverside, where he was to speak on the "pro" side of "Does In-Home Medicine Have a Place in Our Society?" He didn't expect to be back until very late, and although Katherine was tempted to tell him to come by anyway, she held her tongue, deciding not to be so greedy. Instead, she thought of him all through the day and hoped he was thinking of her. Sudden warm flushes spread over her entire body at the oddest times. She could almost feel the touch of him against her skin, his heated breath along the curve of her neck. Katherine reveled in this new, exquisite kind of torture.

She took a long walk in the early morning and then drove into Arrowhead to buy some ski pants and a jacket. After lunch Janet Shea picked her up and took her cabin-hunting. The scene between Katherine and Joe at the reunion had titillated Janet's curiosity, and, true to her straightforward disposition, she had lost no time getting to the heart of the matter.

"What's going on with you and Joe, my girl?" The car door had barely closed before Janet raised an inquiring brow. "You can't breeze in here and snatch up our most eligible bachelor without notice, you know. Andy says I'm to mind my own business, but I can't stand the suspense. Are the two of you—as they say in the gossip magazines— an item?"

Katherine settled back and looked out the window, tempted to give in to a perverse longing to keep it to herself for a little longer. Then her head turned slightly and she gazed at Janet's smiling, open face.

"Yes . . ." Katherine laughed shortly. "I suppose you could say we're an item. Well," she corrected the statement slightly, "maybe only a few lines right now, but I'm working on extending it into a least a paragraph."

"Good for you!" Janet hooted cheerfully. "That man needs a little romance in his life. He was getting downright testy at times. But isn't that just like a man?" She made a clucking sound. "He's got his work and that house he thinks no one knows about and he's got himself convinced his life is ordered and full. I tell you, Katie— seeing him as much as I do—I was really beginning to worry about him."

"Mother Janet," Katherine pronounced teasingly. "You could find something or someone to worry about if you were living in Shangri-la. But," she added, narrowing a more serious gaze at Janet, "speaking of being concerned about someone else, are you sure you should be out and about like this?"

"Like what?" Janet's dark eyes registered sincere bewilderment.

"Janet!" Katherine shook her head in exasperation. "You're so big, your belly is rubbing against the steering wheel. You look like you're ready to explode at any minute, and that sweater you're wearing doesn't look heavy enough to keep a summer chill off!"

"Feel this." Janet reached over and laid her hand over Katherine's. "Toasty, huh?" She waited for Katherine's surprised nod of agreement. "The minute I got pregnant, it was like I had hot water running through my veins. The summer was awful, I can tell you. Andy says I radiate so much heat he's going to keep me pregnant every winter to cut back on fuel bills. Honestly, if I was wearing anything more than a sweater, I'd be sweating like a roasted pig. And as for the other—well, I'm not due for another week, according to Joe. But if I do go into labor, we can just pull over there to the side of the road, okay?"

"Oh." Katherine shuddered at the thought. "Don't even joke about it! Really, Janet. Please don't do anything unexpected. I'd be useless in an emergency. Why don't we just turn around and head back to Rimforest?"

"Not on your life!" Janet refused emphatically. "I've got a place to show you—just came up in the multiple listings this morning—and you won't believe it! I remember it from about five years ago when the original owners sold it. We're almost there."

Janet guided the car off the main highway onto a narrow street that had yet to be snow-plowed.

Like everyone else who lived on the mountain, the Sheas had equipped their car with snow tires and four-wheel drive, so as Janet navigated the curves and turns of the road slowly, there was little danger of sliding off to the side. Still, Katherine was a bit concerned and didn't take her eyes off the road until Janet braked and came to a stop at the bottom of a sloping driveway.

At its crest sat the cutest little dollhouse of a log cabin Katherine had ever seen. The two women got out of the car and walked around the side of the cabin to a front door that was bordered with red trim. Janet opened the door with her master key and they stepped inside.

The walls were covered entirely with varnished knotty pine. The floors were hardwood and covered by braided rugs. It was a small cabin—one bedroom and a loft—but the many large windows made it seem open and airy. The previous owners had removed all their furniture and Katherine found herself mentally decorating the place. The windows and sliding glass door at the front of the cabin opened to an unobstructed view of tiny Green Valley Lake.

Charming. Katherine used the only word she could think of to describe the cabin and how she felt about it. Perfectly charming.

Later, after Jane thad dropped her off and Katherine had settled in front of the fire in her rented cabin at the Retreat, she found herself alternately dozing and daydreaming, a practice she normally did not engage in. But then, she was doing quite a few unfamiliar things lately.

How wonderful, Katherine mused lazily, to escape every weekend to a cabin like that. Large enough for my needs but small enough to discourage weekend visitors. I could leave directly after the taping on Friday afternoon and stay until late Sunday night. And best of all, I could spend every weekend with Joe.

Without—the thought sneaked in uninvited—the troublesome commitment that staying at *his* house would entail. Her own place, and Joe, too—who could want more?

That was the last thing Katherine remembered thinking before falling into a sleep that took her through dinnertime and on to the morning. When she awoke, after sixteen hours of heavy, dreamless slumber, Katherine felt bloated and fuzzy. A cool shower awakened her senses somewhat. Breakfast helped even more. But there was still an annoying residue of something Katherine could not quite identify, an odd sense of foreboding mingled with the nagging question of what had pushed her into a long, nearly comalike sleep.

Still, she was humming tunelessly as she slipped on the shiny new powder-blue ski pants she'd bought the day before. The matching jacket, emblazoned with what resembled a deep purple lightning bolt, zipped form-fitting and snug at the waist over a turtleneck of the same color. Katherine's long, pale hair was tucked up inside a dark purple knit cap whose color added new depth to her warm brown eyes.

As she made a quick check of her appearance, Katherine was more than pleased at how healthy and athletic she looked. In truth, she was a bit apprehensive about their plans for the day. Joe was forgoing his usual Wednesday plans to work on the house and instead was picking Katherine up early for a day of skiing farther up the mountain.

She hadn't maneuvered her way down a slope for years, but she would have to be tortured before she'd ever admit it. She would, she decided halfheartedly, wing it. Wasn't it like riding a bicycle? Once learned, never really forgotten?

It had seemed like such a good idea at the time, tucked into the strong curve of Joe's arms as he told her she would hardly recognize the old ski areas of Snow Summit and Goldmine. He talked of the sun in their faces and the wind at their backs, and for a moment—just long enough for her to say it sounded like a marvelous idea— Katherine forgot that even on her best day she had never really been very good. Joe, of course, was one of those "breakneck" skiers, the kind who barrel down a mountain at full speed, always on the edge of disaster, and emerge without so much as a ding on their skis. The sort who go all day, resenting the time it takes for a lunch break, and then moan when the night lights are turned off.

If I get out of this without a broken leg, Katherine vowed as she looked out the window and watched Joe pull into the parking lot below, *I swear I'll buy Girl Scout cookies without flinching for five years!*

Joe's kiss was long and deep and she melted into his arms, wondering if perhaps she might suggest another way in which they could spend the day. But the notion lost some steam when she realized eventually they would have to get out of bed and face the world anyway.

"You're looking good, Katie." Joe smiled gently, his finger tracing the contours of her cheek. He tipped her chin and placed another, lighter kiss on her mouth. "Taste good, too."

She blushed slightly, amazed, basking in the glow of Joe's admiration. How did he do that? She could count on the fingers of one hand the times she'd blushed over the years, and in twelve days he had her going on and off like the red warning light outside the stage door.

"I'm ready." Katherine's voice was filled with joyous laughter. "You look pretty dazzling yourself, doctor. I like a man with good buns." Her hand snaked over the gray waterproof material of his ski pants and patted him lightly. "I guess after a full, sensuous mouth and sparkling eyes, good buns are the first thing I look for in my men."

Joe grinned and nodded in agreement. "I've always been kind of proud of them myself. But as much as I'd like to stand here discussing my anatomy, I think we'd best get going or there won't be any clean snow left."

Katherine swallowed hard and forced a smile as Joe threw open the door and waited for her to gather up her purse and sunglasses. The sunlight was behind him, shooting golden streaks across his light brown hair and outlining his powerful body with a kind of bright white aura. He was dressed more casually than she, in gray pants and a burgundy jacket with navy-blue turtleneck worn more for warmth than style. Still, he looked as though he *belonged* on the mountain. Not, Katherine pondered the thought guiltily, like a transplanted city slicker just stepped off the runway of a fashion show.

No! Katherine admonished herself sharply. *I will not do this to myself!* I will not look for reasons to ruin the happiness I feel!

She leaned into the arm that Joe had draped casually across her shoulders and walked beside him out to the car. The drive up the mountain to Big Bear passed quickly in a blur of small talk and an occasional intimate glance that passed between them like an electric current.

The parking lot at Snow Summit was already nearly full. The deck of the central lodge, Summit Inn, was teeming with brightly clad skiers milling between the restaurant and sport shop and the sidewalks leading to the various lifts—six doubles, one triple, and three surface lifts serving one hundred ten acres of runs that sounded progressively dangerous as Joe named them for her: Upper Log Chute, the Wall, and, most ominous of all, the Olympic. Some of the runs were over a mile long from summit station to base.

"Don't they have something called a baby slope?" Katherine spoke to the top of Joe's head as he bent to help her on with the ski boots they'd just rented.

"Sure." Joe laughed before the reason for the quiver in her voice hit him. "Been a long time, has it?" He lifted Katherine from the chair and hugged her tightly. "Why didn't you say so before?" Her pained, hopeful expression was answer enough. "You don't have to be perfect, you know," he whispered softly. "This isn't some television script where no one ever blows their noses or goes to the bathroom. We're talking real life here, Katie. You don't have to be perfect," he repeated, "and neither do I."

They started on the beginners' slope and Katherine relearned the basics with surprising speed and determination. From snowplow, the first turn a skier learns, she quickly progressed to a stem christie and within an hour was traversing the gentle slope at a speed that prompted the instructors to request that she and Joe move on to a more advanced run. At noontime, deaf to Joe's pleas that she slow down and take it easy, Katherine was schussing down a lesser run with an exuberance that surprised them both. Finally he had to drag her off to the side and stand over her, practically force-feeding her the sandwiches he had tucked into the zippered pockets of his jacket.

"You go on, Joe," Katherine urged while she munched on a tasteless bite of the inn's packaged sandwich. "I don't want to hold you back. I know you want to hit one of the better runs. Go on." She looked at her watch. "We can meet back here in two hours, okay?" She was already on her feet, adjusting the wrist straps of her ski poles and straightening her sunglasses over the bridge of her nose. "Really," she insisted, "this is great but not exactly a team sport, so you go on and pick me up later."

So that he wouldn't have a chance to protest,

Katherine pushed out her left heel, placed her left ski at an angle, and shifted her weight, using her poles to push off in the direction of the run. As she gained speed, the snow under her skis sprayed over her boots, and as Joe had promised, she felt the crisp wind and warm sun on her face. It was a glorious feeling.

After tackling the Olympic run five times in two hours, Joe returned to the summit station on the lower run where Katherine had said to meet her. He waited fifteen minutes and might have missed seeing her completely except that during a final sweep of the area before going down to the base, Joe noticed a pale blue lump at the edge of a narrow grouping of sugar pines. He side-stepped, edging his skis at an angle to the slope until he was standing over her prone, spread-eagled body.

"Katie?" He bent anxiously over her, relief flooding his face when she opened her eyes at the sound of his voice.

"Katie is dead," she intoned grimly. Her gloved hands gathered fistsfuls of snow, which she tossed listlessly atop her chest. "Katherine Mallory is deceased," she repeated. "The kindest gesture would be to bury me now and put me out of my misery."

Chuckling sympathetically, Joe leaned over to help Katherine to her feet. "Come on, you panty-waist, it's only a few hundred feet to the bottom. Let's go."

"I can't," Katherine whined. "Every muscle in my body has atrophied. I can't move."

A long groan shuddered from between her lips

as Joe set her upright. With his arm locked around her waist for support, he traversed in a zigzag pattern down the hill. He then unsnapped the bindings of Katherine's skis and guided her onto the observation deck of the Bear Bottom Lodge. While he was gone off in the direction of the snack bar, Katherine slumped into the deck chair. With the last vestiges of her energy she pulled another chair close and lifted each agonizingly cramped leg onto its seat. When Joe returned with two Styrofoam cups of hot cocoa, he found her stretched out like a lizard basking on a rock.

"I *told* you to take it easy," Joe reminded her ungraciously as he pried open her fingers and then closed them again around the warm cup.

Katherine opened her eyes, fixing him with a baleful stare. "If you *really* loved me," she said, unthinkingly using the well-worn phrase, "you'd have taken better care of me. You'd have knocked me down and *made* me stop tearing up and down that mountain like a stupid ninny."

"I *do* love you," Joe replied gently, so casually that Katherine had to think about it twice to be certain he had really said it. "But you're a big girl, Katie," he continued as though he hadn't just uttered four little words that shook Katherine to the core of her being. "You have to make your own choices. My God, girl"—his fingers closed lightly over her thigh—"your muscles are more twisted than one of Ma Bell's telephone-receiver cords! Relax. I'll take you back to my place and give you a brisk rubdown with my best horse liniment."

"Sounds good," Katherine admitted with a

trembling smile. "But, uh, first, could you back it up a little? To, you know, that part where you said you love me?"

Joe laughed without a trace of inhibition, as though the time and place for his declaration were perfectly natural. "Would it have been better with champagne and violins? Sorry, but it just felt right. Are you sorry I said it? I can't take it back or change it, but I don't have to mention it again."

"At least not more than three or four times a day, if you don't mind." Katherine suppressed a flinch as she lifted her hand to Joe's face. "I don't think I can take too much of the way my heart turns over when I hear you say it." She stared wide-eyed, reveling in the sight of him, as Joe leaned closer to brush a soft, lingering kiss against her mouth.

"I love you, Joey." It was only after he had leaned back again that Katherine noticed the hand that held her cocoa had gone limp and the hot fluid was dribbling over the rim and onto her new ski pants.

Fifteen minutes later they were stretched out in chairs, side by side, with just their fingers touching and both their faces raised to the late-afternoon sun.

"I think," Katherine murmured lazily as she stifled a yawn, "you're going to have to dynamite me out of this chair."

"Hm-m-m." Joe didn't even bother to open his eyes. "I guess we should think about getting back to my place, but . . ."

"Speaking of 'my' place," Katherine said, brightening despite her physical discomfort, "I have something to tell you. I think Janet and I have found the perfect weekend cabin, just over in Green Valley. I've been mulling it over since yesterday and I think I'll buy it. I really need a place, a permanent place, I can run away to after working all week and . . ." She couldn't help but notice Joe's fingers had stopped caressing her own. Katherine faltered a moment and then went on, ". . . and you and I will have weekends together, holidays, any time I can get away from the studio."

"Actually," Joe said slowly, as though weighing his words carefully, "I have something more than just weekends and holidays in mind."

"Such as?" The dread, the hesitation in Katherine's voice was evident. Now, she thought sinkingly, here it comes. The ultimatum. All or nothing.

"Well, like you said, permanence." Joe's answer rang in her head like a death knell. "A real honest-to-God relationship. You know, waking up in the morning together, going to sleep at night together. Depending on one another, sharing. Gold rings, vows, children, everything. *Being together.*"

"At what cost?" Katherine snapped before she could control her irritation. "My career? I can't possibly make the drive every day on and off this mountain, and you've made it abundantly clear how you feel about living anywhere close to the city. What do you expect me to do? Walk away from everything I've worked so hard to achieve, from my life?" Katherine's voice raised uncontrollably as she expressed all the thoughts that had been tormenting her from the moment she had acknowledged their feelings for each other as more than just a casual affair. "Why does it have to be *me*, and not you, who has to give something up in order to have something else?"

"I don't know," Joe answered truthfully. "Maybe because I've found my purpose here and if I walk away, I leave myself behind."

"Oh, I see," Katherine retorted caustically. "Fifteen years on *Bright Promise* is nothing compared to your selfless profession. You—"

"That isn't what I meant, Katie. Don't put words into my mouth. I'm only suggesting that perhaps you would find *another* life-style more suited to your needs. You were less than content when you came here, if you remember."

"*That* is ridiculous." He was hitting close to home now and it made her even more defensive. "I was under pressure, that's all. I hadn't had a real vacation in years." She sat up and took her feet off the chair, making a big show of adjusting her jacket, bending over to remove the rented ski boots, anything to keep from looking directly at Joe.

He would have none of it. Locking his hand under her chin, he tilted Katherine's face to his and gazed deeply into her eyes. "I'm only offering what it's in my power to give, Katie. I won't make any promises or compromises I know I won't be able to keep later."

"I knew it!" Katherine sagged into his arms and whispered accusingly into the softness of his jacket, just loud enough so that he had to strain to hear her, "I knew you were going to do this to me. Straight-arrow Joe. Why couldn't we just keep it simple and light? Uncomplicated." Tears welled in her eyes as she looked pleadingly up at him. "I only have a few more days before I have to go back to L.A. Can't we just spend them together and take it a little at a time? Can't that be enough, for now?"

"Bits and pieces are never enough when you love someone as much as I love you, Katie." Joe slowly pulled the knit cap off Katherine's head, and as her pale hair tumbled to her shoulders, he buried his face in the soft curve of her neck, breathing in the scent of her. "But I can't give up even that."

Silent now, Joe stood and reached out his hands to Katherine. She grasped them and he lifted her out of the chair. His arm went tightly around her shoulders, hugging her close as they walked, troubled and uncertain, from the sunbathed deck.

Chapter Eight

❧

"Oh-h-h, that feels so good!" Katherine moaned and pressed her hips farther into the bed. "Don't stop! Yes, *there*. Oh, that's wonderful!"

"I *should* be offended," Joe growled with a frown. "You never say anything like that when we're making love!" He paused a moment, applying more liniment to his hands before going back to massaging the exact spot on Katherine's shoulder that had caused her to call out. When he started, she was tense and knotted. Now he had managed to rub her into a near-catatonic state. She smelled of peppermint and the fumes were beginning to sting his eyes. Joe rested back on his heels, his legs straddling either side of Katherine's naked thighs. The potbellied stove in his bedroom was going full blast so he was stripped to the waist as he leaned over her body and worked his fingers into her aching muscles.

She thought of that sight as she lay on her stomach, of how she had watched the smooth, taut cords snake across Joe's shoulders and arms before he'd flipped her over and began massaging her back. As he bent to the task, there wasn't

even the slightest bulge where the waistband of
his jeans encircled his stomach.

"That ought to do you for a while." Joe's open
palm came down with a playful smack on Katherine's buttocks as he rolled off and stretched out
beside her. "Next time, I'll make sure you don't
overdo, even if I have to follow you all over the
mountain. That," he said, breaking off the lecture with a smirk, "isn't an idea I find totally
repugnant." His fingers danced lightly over
Katherine's spine and came to rest just in the
hollow of her lower back. "But if you're concerned,
I'll be happy—in my professional capacity, of
course—to conduct another complete examina-
tion at this time if it will—"

"Never mind." Katherine slithered quickly off
the bed and reached for a terry-cloth bathrobe
hanging on a knob inside the closet. As she folded
it over her body and tightened the belt at her
waist, she watched Joe closely.

*How can we be talking and joking back and
forth when what we both really want is to get
back to the conversation we were having at Big
Bear this afternoon?*

Katherine was the one with the Emmys sitting
inside a display case in her living room, but she
was convinced Joe was every bit the performer
she had worked most of her life to become. He
wasn't going to bring up the subject again. Like
Katherine, he was just going to foolishly avoid it
and hope that it would somehow miraculously
solve itself.

That, of course, was not likely to happen. And
they both knew it. Later, Katherine promised

herself; we'll talk about it later. I can't bear to think about what I'll say, and Joe doesn't want to face what he will hear. Just a few more happy hours and then we'll talk about it.

"I'm going downstairs to mutilate some eggs," she announced brightly. "Want to come and peer over my shoulder?" Without waiting for an answer, Katherine spun on her heel and walked out of the bedroom. Every step was an agony of clenching muscles and stiff joints.

She grabbed hold of the railing on the stairs and supported herself as she limped down, step by step. Joe called out something in her wake, something about not babying herself or her legs would tighten up even more.

Katherine paused on the stairs and looked behind her, tossing back a scathing glare she hoped would penetrate the walls and hit Joe like a laser blast. Know-it-all! She could barely keep from whimpering as she continued her descent of the stairs.

If he's so smart, Katherine thought smugly, how come I still feel so lousy?

Her hand groped along the wall at the bottom of the stairs until she found the switch for the overhead light. The kitchen was neat as a pin, everything in its place, the counter spotless and shiny, and not a single dirty dish in the sink.

Who could live with such a man? she asked herself with a flash of irrational anger. The obvious comparsion burned brightly in her mind— the casual, thoughtless disarray of her own home, where a coat always seemed to be dropped over the chair, magazines were always scattered about, and the makeup on the bathroom counter never seemed to get put away.

We two, she decided adamantly, would drive each other up the wall inside a week.

The refrigerator was stocked with the kind of food Katherine shunned on her bimonthly excursions to the supermarket. Italian olives, a nearly empty bottle of capers, marinated artichoke crowns, Dijon mustard, a big jar of wheat germ. What did he do with all this stuff? Aside from a head of iceberg lettuce, a few tomatoes, and a half-dozen pieces of fruit, Katherine's grocery list was solely made up of frozen, precooked meals neatly packaged in compartmented aluminum plates. And vitamins. Lots of them, to supplement what she was missing in her diet.

On a hunch, Katherine opened several cabinets and found what she was seeking. A *single* bottle of full-spectrum vitamins, the kind you take once a day on the off-chance you've somehow missed something. She replaced the bottle and slammed the cabinet shut so ferociously the dishes in the adjoining cabinet shook and clattered.

As quickly as the irritation had surfaced, it faded away and she bent over the counter, resting her forehead in her hands.

What am I getting so angry about? Katherine rubbed her temples soothingly. Does it really matter that Joe's eating habits are better than mine? Or that he skies better than I do? And he gets out-of-doors more often? Cooks better? Keeps a neater house?

Did Joe really make her feel inadequate, or was he just the catalyst that forced her to confront and yearn for the things that were missing in her own life? Katherine had no desire to compete with Joe, to outshine him. There was no "anything you can do, I can do better" curse upon her lips. Then what? What was it that made her ache—?

"Hey!" The sound of Joe's voice floating down from the loft interrupted Katherine's thoughts. "I don't smell anything down there but the lingering scent of peppermint. What's going on?"

"I'm hobbling as fast as I can," Katherine replied. She took her anxiety and uneasiness and folded them neatly inside a box. She shut the lid gently, closing it off until another time. "Did you hear that?" She rattled the shelves inside the refrigerator as she reached for a carton of eggs. "And that?" A large black cast-iron skillet clattered atop the range. "What time is it?"

"Nearly eight," Joe reported, the muffled padding of his slippered feet sounding on the stairs. He'd tied a kimono-type robe loosely over his jeans. He stopped briefly at the kitchen door before being waved away by Katherine as she returned her attention to the cluttered counter.

Eggs were one food staple she'd learned her way around. A little parsley, some cheese, a few spices, a touch of milk, a pat of butter, and—presto—a moist, fluffy omelet!

Twenty minutes later they were seated at the table, enjoying her culinary efforts. And judging by the way Joe ate everything except the small portion Katherine served herself, his compliments were not just empty words.

Katherine smiled, remembering how, as a child,

her mother had cooked something with a peculiar texture and smell and, when told to at least try it, Katherine had poked it around her plate with a fork, spreading it thin so it looked half-eaten. Or, when that trick no longer worked, how she had deposited small mouthfuls of some hated food under the flared rim of her plate when her parents weren't looking. Later, when it came time to perform her nightly chore of clearing and washing the dishes, Katherine would lift her own plate off the table and there, atop the plastic table mat, lay a half-moon of uneaten food that she would quickly brush into a dishcloth and throw away. She could still see her mother's face when *that* ploy was discovered, still hear the lecture about starving children all over the world.

"What are you smiling so secretly about?" Joe wiped his mouth and laid the napkin on the table, pushing back on two legs of the chair as his hands folded over his stomach. "You look pretty satisfied with yourself."

"No." Katherine laughed shortly and began gathering up the plates. "I was just thinking about what devils children can be."

"Let me do that." Joe took the dishes from her hands and nudged Katherine back to her chair. "Cooks never clear off the fruits of their labor. It's a rule, carved somewhere on the back of a roasting pan." He disappeared into the kitchen and then returned for a second load. "I don't know about you, but *I* was a wonderful child. My mother," he said lifting a brow in a haughty, self-satisfied gesture, "says I never gave her a moment's worry."

"Your mother," Katherine retorted sweetly, "Must be thinking of some other child, in another life, perhaps. Either that or all those years living with you pushed her around the bend."

"I'm going to tell her you think she's crazy, the next time I see her," Joe threatened wickedly.

When he retreated into the kitchen, Katherine listened to the sound of running water for a minute and then got up and wandered in to find Joe washing and drying the dishes.

"Do you suffer from some kind of neatness fixation?" She glanced at the counters, already cleared away and spotlessly clean. "Can't this wait until the morning?"

Joe pretended to shudder. "I hate waking up a dried eggs and milk-rimmed glasses. Besides, all bachelors are compulsively neat. We wait until we get married to fall apart and start throwing T-shirts and underwear on the floor." He looked back over his shoulder and leered. "Why don't you go spread yourself out seducutively by the fire? I'll join you in a minute."

When he did join her—and it *was* only a few minutes—Joe found Katherine sitting close to the fire, knees drawn up under the bathrobe and pressed against her chest, warming her bare feet near the flame. Silently she lifted a hand and slipped it into his. He stood for a moment watching her with incredibly blue, troubled eyes and then sat down beside her.

This is it. Katherine read Joe's expression correctly. This is where we stop the small talk and the friendly dancing around every topic of conversation except the one that's been on both our minds all evening.

I don't want to hear this. She swallowed hard and fought back a sudden rise of hysteria. Please, Joey! Don't force me to make a choice neither one of us is going to like.

Joe moved slightly and then hesitated as though he had heard Katherine's silent plea. His arm went around her shoulders and hugged her gently to his chest. His lips pressed against her hair, and in the end, it was Katherine who started the confrontation she'd been dreading.

"I'm *not* giving up my work," she blurted out, blond hair swinging from side to side as she shook her head emphatically. She jerked her shoulders free of his arm, and using her feet for leverage, scooted back beyond his reach. Her arms clasped her knees tightly to her chest in a defiant, untouchable gesture.

"I didn't ask you to do that." Joe regained his calm quickly after the surprise of Katherine's sudden outburst.

"Oh?" She inclined her head and smiled bitterly. "What do you call it, then? You said you wanted marriage and children. Correct me if I'm wrong, but I thought you meant to include me in those plans."

"Of course I meant you!" Joe's tone mirrored Katherine's sarcasm.

"Well," she continued, arching a brow deliberately, "aside from being the least romantic proposal I've ever received, the implications are pretty clear. You want to marry me but you won't live with me in L.A. You want me, but only on *your* terms."

"I'm trying to be realistic, Katie," Joe defended himself. "How many of those so-called 'Hollywood marriages' ever work out? Name just a half-dozen and we can put a halt to this right now and I'll go along with anything you want."

"Paul Newman and Joanne Woodward!" Katherine immediately came up with the finest example her business had to offer. "Ruth Gordon and Garson Kanin. Ah ..." She was losing ground quickly. "Ah, Ricardo Montalban has been married to the same woman for years. And, uh ... Oh, this is stupid! What have other people's marriages got to do with *us*?"

"Nothing," Joe admitted. "But I don't think a marriage, a lasting marriage, has a good chance under the conditions we'd have to deal with if you weren't willing to put our relationship ahead of everything else. Part-time marriage sounds tempting and convenient, but I don't think it has any basis in reality. And I *know* you can't raise children by long distance."

"You are really one to talk, Joe Mercer," Katherine retorted in a huff. "Office hours, hospital duty, emergencies—"

"Which is precisely why I choose to practice my profession *here*. I'll never be rich, but I'll also never burn out. Medicine consumes only about a third of my time. The rest I'm prepared to offer my wife and children. Katie, I love you, but I won't kid myself into believing that love is enough to keep it all together."

"Why does it feel like you're forcing me to give

up *my* life in order to share yours?" The resentment and anger had drained out of her and she felt hollow and hopeless inside.

"I don't mean to do that, Katie." Joe moved close to her and lifted a hand to stroke her face. "Maybe I'm trying too hard to protect myself. I guess the truth is, I can't stand the thought of losing you all over again. Maybe I'm holding on too tightly."

Katherine saw the opening and sprang on it eagerly. "We can *make* it work, Joe. I know we can. If you'll just give it a chance, I know we can find a way to have it all." She could see the skepticism in his face even as he nodded his willingness to hear her out. "All right," Katherine acknowledged reluctantly, "maybe ours *isn't* the best of circumstances. But how can we be sure if we don't at least try?" Again she waited for some sign from Joe that he was carefully weighing her argument. "For the time being, I can buy that cabin I saw yesterday and I'll come up on weekends. Every weekend, I promise!" As she said it, Katherine realized it didn't sound like very much, even to her. "I keep hearing it isn't the quantity of time spent together but the quality of that time that really matters."

Joe chuckled, a humorless sound. "Whoever said that is obviously too busy to let anything or anyone get in the way. How about 'out of sight, out of mind'?"

"'Absence makes the heart grow fonder,'" Katherine shot back with a timorous smile.

Joe grimaced and struggled to his feet, still a

long way from being convinced. "There's always the old standby, 'when all else fails, make love' "

Katherine looked up at him and giggled. "I've never heard that cliché in quite the same context." She sobered quietly as a tiny spark ignited deep inside her at the memory of how all thought vanished from her mind when Joe's hands and mouth possessed her, when he touched and aroused her.

Joe pulled Katherine to her feet and stood holding her for a moment, his hands gliding slowly across her back, each movement pressing her closer against the hardness of his own body.

Katherine closed her eyes, reveling in the sensation of losing herself inside him. She moaned softly and stood on tiptoe, her arms wrapped tightly around his neck. A quiver surged through her as she felt Joe's breath quicken against her throat.

His fingers slipped between their bodies and undid the belt around Katherine's waist, parting the robe with a languidness that was tantalizing. Joe's hands moved inside the robe, starting at Katherine's hips and moving to the curving hollow of her slim waist and then up slowly, lightly, until her breasts were cupped within his hands, warm and trembling at his touch.

Joe's thumbs brushed over the taut nipples as he bent to kiss Katherine's open mouth. His teeth closed over her bottom lip, pulling at it with an agonizing gentleness.

Then, with a smile that belied the urgency of his own passion, Joe returned his arm to Kath-

erine's waist and led her toward the stairs that
went up to the sleeping loft.

The terry-cloth robe fluttered at her sides, ex-
posing a wide slit of creamy skin from neck to
ankles as she walked beside him. The feel of
Joe's arm around her, the touch of his flesh against
hers, the intimacy and uninhibitedness with
which she basked in his sidelong glances, all
combined to prompt a soft, purely sensual sigh
that caught in her throat as they mounted the
stairs.

Within minutes they stood naked before one
another, their bodies illuminated by the solitary
golden-orange glow from the cast-iron stove in
the corner of the room.

For the first time, Katherine was able to see
and appreciate how truly strong and handsome
Joe's body was. Wide, corded shoulders tapered
to a slim waist, and a band of baby-fine hair—
darker that the sun-streaked hair on his head—
trailed from his chest to just below his navel. His
legs were beautifully proportioned, straight and
muscular.

Katherine's eyes feasted on the sight of him.
Her hands tentatively rested at his hips, and
then, growing bolder, danced lightly downward,
fingers closing around him, stroking as Joe's body
convulsed with response.

He clasped her to him and swung her in a
half-circle toward the bed, using an arm at her
back to soften the descent. She was captured
beneath him when he flung a long leg over her
thighs. He nuzzled the hollow of her neck, his
mouth blazing a trail of moist heat from Kath-

erine's throat to the rosy tip of her breast. There he teased and sucked until Katherine groaned aloud with pleasure.

Her hands sought him out again, mesmerized by the velvety smoothness. She felt his lips move up to claim hers, his tongue hot and demanding. Katherine arched her back instinctively, seeking a release from the overpowering pressure that began deep in the core of her and spread like fire to the very tips of every nerve in her body.

Joe answered her insistent plea, his knee moving between her legs, hands slipping under her hips, lifting her to receive him. Katherine sighed with satisfaction as Joe entered and filled her. Her legs wrapped around his back and she clung to him greedily. His thrusts rocked her body, bringing her to the edge and then withdrawing and beginning all over again. A sound like strangled laughter erupted from deep within her chest and she reveled in the prolonged ecstasy until, finally, the passion rolled over them like a cresting wave and they lay spent and quiet in each other's arms.

Chapter Nine

Four o'clock in the morning was still too early for traffic. Except for an occasional delivery truck, Katherine was all alone on the narrow highway that led down the mountain, and for a time her thoughts were diverted by the chilly darkness that engulfed her. She drove slowly and cautiously along the dimly lit, snaking curves of the road, her eyes wide and filled with apprehension. For the most part, the southbound lane hugged the mountain, but her mind was full of gruesome images—of skidding and drifting across the highway, of plowing through the two-foot-high guardrail and dropping off the side of mountain. And the very real fear of a sudden crippling snowstorm.

Katherine's heart pounded like a hammer in her chest. Her fingers gripped the steering wheel so tightly her knuckles ached.

She was just at the point of tearful admonitions—you shouldn't have sneaked away like a thief in the night—when she rounded a bend and the lights of San Bernardino twinkled up into her vision. An audible sigh of relief echoed inside the Mercedes.

Katherine relaxed her desperate grasp on the wheel and leaned forward slightly to peer out at the road ahead. There were no piles of dirty gray slush pushed off to the side of the highway. She was on dry ground again and the nightmare visions and fears her mind had conjured up to keep her company on the tortuous drive away from Rimforest were quickly and thankfully forgotten.

Static sounds of crackling and buzzing filled the car as Katherine fiddled with the radio dial, trying to find a little soothing music to accompany her on the long drive back to L.A. But with the panic of road conditions dissipated, a kind of drowsiness settled behind her eyes, so she changed her mind and tuned in a rock station instead, bringing up the volume to jar her senses.

While she was still maneuvering the bottom part of the mountain, it was easy not to think about what she had just done. But once Katherine made the turn onto the monotonous strip of freeway at San Bernardino, her mind relaxed and she could no longer keep the persistent thoughts at bay.

Joe slept like a hibernating bear. His arms and legs had been tangled up in hers and he had not even stirred when Katherine slowly extracted herself and slipped out of bed. She had dressed quickly in the dark and then tiptoed down the stairs, pausing in her flight only long enough to hastily scribble a note of inadequate explanation.

"Darling Joe," the note read, "I can't think or make any decision being here so close to you. I am going back to L.A. to settle my contract with the network and will probably work with writers through the weekend. Will call you soon and will definitely see your face in nine days."

Without thinking, Katherine had signed the note with a large, swirling K, an impersonal and automatic gesture she used in most of her correspondence. Now the wording of the message and the signature seemed to Katherine as loving and intimate as a grocery list.

With the note taped to the refrigerator door, Katherine had quietly slipped outside. A split-second decision was all that was needed before she dismissed the idea of getting to her car through the shrubs along the side of the house. Katherine hunched her shoulders forward, bracing herself against the cold and wind, and started off down the alley and around the block.

Once inside her car, she turned the key in the ignition and the Mercedes purred smoothly to life and she drove to the Retreat. There she packed her bags quickly and put a personal check inside an envelope provided by the Retreat. After her luggage was in the car, Katherine slipped the envelope under the office door with a "thank-you" scrawled across the front.

And now she was speeding past Ontario and Alta Loma on her way to Los Angeles. As the sun rose behind her, the freeway began to fill with commuters and the flow of traffic started to slow. Katherine yawned and gave her head a quick shake to dispel the exhaustion that was creeping over her like a blanket.

She *was* doing the right thing, for herself and for Joe. The note was a coward's way out, but she never could have left if she'd had to face him. This way, they would both have the time they needed to weigh carefully the commitment discussed between them. Although he had acquiesced somewhat, Katherine had seen the doubt in Joe's eyes when she'd insisted they could work out the differences of their careers and life-styles.

For all her brave and optimistic assurances, Katherine had her own share of doubts. In the very beginning, the first time he'd kissed her, Katherine had known instinctively that this man was going to want more from her than she was prepared to give. And, strangely enough, Joe had never once tried to hide the truth of her fears. He *did* want too much. He wanted everything.

A person would have to be crazy, Katherine grumbled out loud, absolutely insane to give up all the advantages her life had to offer.

Forget the money; it was almost indecent to even think of the hefty salary she received. What about rubbing shoulders with some of the most famous people in the world? And the fame she herself enjoyed? Why, her name alone was enough to ensure a good table at any of Hollywood's finest restaurants. And, all right, consider the money! Katherine had enough of it to buy anything that took her fancy. Wasn't she driving around in a thirty-thousand-dollar Mercedes? Wearing designer clothes? Living in a penthouse apartment?

Insane! Katherine touched the turn indicator and eased the car into the far left lane toward the Hollywood freeway. The traffic was now bumper-to-bumper and it took her almost an hour to get from the turnoff to the Cahuenga Boulevard off-ramp. She turned right and drove over the rolling hills for several miles and then turned right again onto Hollyview Avenue. Ten-story apartment buildings loomed ahead of her. She pulled into a driveway, guiding the car down to the guard booth and gate that led to high-security subterranean parking beneath the building. The guard recognized her, pressed a button that released the steel gates, and waved her through. With the instinct of a homing pigeon, Katherine zipped along the shadowy corridors. The sound of the car's tires was a shrill whine against the smooth concrete. She came to a stop three spaces away from the underground elevator. Taking just her makeup bag, Katherine got out of the car and limped toward the elevator, leaning against the cool metal as she waited for it to descend. The door pulled back and she came face to face with a woman she had seen a hundred times since moving into the building. But still there was that cautious, guarded smile and nothing more as the woman stepped out of the elevator and Katherine walked in. As the elevator door closed again and she pressed the number ten, Katherine suddenly realized that she had never taken the time or made the effort to know anyone in her building. After almost two years, she was still at the smile-and-nod stage.

Katherine stepped out on the top floor of the building, a floor that housed only two spacious apartments, including her own. When she opened the door to her apartment, Katherine noticed immediately that her cleaning lady had been in and straightened the havoc Katherine had left before going up to Rimforest. She made a mental note to give Betty an extra bonus, and solemnly promised to stop behaving like a messy four-year-old before staggering down the hall to her bedroom.

The gray-blue satin comforter on her bed had never looked more fluffy and inviting. In fact, the entire room had the cool, tomblike air of sanctuary about it. Katherine unplugged the telephone and stretched out, drawing the corners of the quilt up over her legs. Her face sank into the softness of matching pillows, and within seconds she drifted into the sought-after haven of tranquil sleep.

Katherine awoke in the late afternoon feeling only slightly better than when she had come in the front door. A long, steamy shower, followed by an agonizing two-minute ice-cold spray, did its part to invigorate her sluggish body. Clad in a silky Japanese kimono, her feet encased in cloth-soled tabis, Katherine padded into the kitchen and, holding little hope, opened the refrigerator door. As she expected, the contents of the refrigerator reflected her two-week absence. Nothing but limp lettuce, a bruised banana, and a carton of deli potato salad with something green and furry growing under the lid.

Uck! Katherine shuddered and tried the freezer compartment. A single can of frozen orange juice fell under her ravenous gaze. It took more energy than she really had, but in a few minutes Katherine had dumped the solid orange block into the blender, added three cans of tap water, and watched as the foaming liquid spun around inside.

Carrying her glass of cold, frothy juice, Katherine crossed the living room and sat down at the desk. She lifted the glass to her lips and drained it in a single motion. Then she reached for the telephone.

Joe's was the only voice she really wanted to hear, but she would be defeating her purpose in being separated from him if the first thing she did was call him. No, it was best if they gave each other a little time alone. Even the thought of him was like a magnet drawing her back to Rimforest.

Katherine shook her head to dispel the sudden images of him that sprang into her mind. Joe standing in the shadows of the high school, silent and brooding. Joe, the tawny glow from the fire shining in his hair. Joe laughing, frowning, teasing.

Katherine's hand trembled as she dialed the number of her answering service. While it rang, she braced the receiver under her chin and opened the middle drawer of the desk to pull our notepaper and a pen. After giving her account number when the service picked up on the other end, Katherine was greeted by a cheery, if somewhat disembodied-sounding voice. "Oh, hi, Miss Mallory. Welcome home. Did you have a nice vacation?"

"Yes, thank you," Katherine responded automatically to the impersonal voice. "But it's back to work now. Did I get any calls while I was gone?"

"Just let me punch up your number. Let's see,

Melanie James called three times about a party she's having Friday night." The switchboard operator rattled off Melanie's number and then proceeded down a list of callers and messages that kept Katherine scribbling furiously for ten minutes. She concluded with, "Your agent called four times this afternoon, insisting you were home. Mr. Michaels said it was urgent, so I rang through but there was no answer."

Katherine thought of the telephone in her bedroom, unplugged while she slept. "In future," she said, remembering the promise she'd made herself, "would you make absolutely certain that no calls are put through, under any circumstances, unless *I* decide whether or not they're important?"

"Certainly, Miss Mallory." The voice took on a slightly miffed tone, as though to imply that Katherine's request was a bit presumptuous.

"Thank you." Katherine spoke crisply, refusing to be intimidated. "Good-bye"—she ended the conversation with a smile—"and have a nice day."

Katherine got up and turned on the stereo, then went to draw the draperies. She opened the sliding glass door and went out on the balcony. Overhead, a depressing cloud of pinkish smog blanketed the sky, obstructing a view that sometimes took in the Hollywood hills and a tiny speck of ocean beyond. Those clear, far-reaching days were fast becoming a reason for celebration. Not like—

No! Katherine stopped herself and hurried back inside the apartment. Comparing Los Angeles to Rimforest was like comparing apples and chocolate éclairs. They were both juicy and yummy but totally different, offering variant delights.

And one, a sneaky inner voice whispered, is better for you.

Katherine squared her shoulders obstinately. She needed something to do, to occupy her time, if she was going to get through the first few hours without placing a desperate, incoherent call to Rimforest's resident sawbones. It was too late in the day to get in any serious shopping, and besides, only a lunatic with a death wish would go out on the streets of Hollywood after dark without an armed guard.

Katherine settled on rearranging the living-room furniture. Looking at it now, she found it hard to believe she had once considered the decor the height of elegance. Why, it was barely livable, it was so sterile.

The entire penthouse was done in gray-blue and off-white with splashes of peach and rose as accent colors. Every inch of the apartment's two thousand square feet was covered with off-white plush carpeting. The furniture, low-slung in the Scandinavian style, was set about sparsely and offset with slender tables and cabinets made entirely of glass and chrome. Once, the color scheme had seemed pristine and restful. Now it was cold and antiseptic, as though too perfect for habitation.

The lights are on, Katherine thought as she hummed an eerie tune, but nobody's home.

She worked hard, pushing and shoving furniture around until fatigue and hunger overtook her. After ordering a home-delivered pizza from a nearby restaurant, Katherine stood back and surveyed her handiwork. She decided she hated it, and after taking some nourishment, would try again.

The important thing was that she had gone three hours straight without thinking of Joe. Well, maybe an errant little thought now and then, but nothing to send her sobbing to the telephone.

I can do this, she decided firmly. I can be away from him during the week, every week. No problem. It'll be even easier when I'm working again. Long hours, tired nights. I can do it.

I'm having trouble sleeping, she reasoned later in the quiet darkness of her bedroom, because I slept most of the afternoon away. Eating that greasy pizza didn't help much, either.

Katherine fumbled in the dark and found the remote control for the television at the foot of her bed. She turned it on and stacked pillows behind her back to make herself more comfortable. Switching channels back and forth, she finally settled on a 1940's melodrama that made her terribly sad.

In the morning, Katherine couldn't remember where the tears had left off and the sleeping had begun. But it didn't matter. The important thing was that she woke up feeling just fine, her old self again, ready to take on the world.

The first order of the day was replenishing the cupboards and refrigerator. Katherine dressed casually, went out to the store, and returned with three shopping bags full of goodies and not one frozen carton in the whole batch.

After breakfast—eggs and bacon prepared in the exact manner she had perfected while staying at the Retreat but that somehow didn't taste nearly as good—Katherine went to the phone and placed a call to Rimforest.

"Janet? Hi, it's Katie."

The voice on the other end of the line sounded breathless and forced. "You slippery thing, you! The way you snuck out of town, I wondered if I'd ever be hearing from you again."

"It *was* a bit sudden, I know," Katherine admitted sheepishly, "but I had some things to take care of, and . . . Is something wrong? You sound a little funny."

"Nothing's wrong." Janet's laughter was low and mellow. "In fact, I couldn't be better. I'm in labor."

"You're *what?*" Katherine nearly dropped the telephone. "In labor? Janet, what are you doing at the office? My God, shouldn't you be at the hospital? Have you called Joe? Where's Andy?"

"Relax, Katie," Janet replied happily. "Everything's under control. It just started an hour ago. Andy's gone back to the house for my suitcase. Joe is ready to meet us at the hospital as soon as the contractions get down to a few minutes apart. And me, well, I'm just sitting here trying to think of something to do to keep my mind off it. So why don't you distract me for a while? Why are you calling?"

"Hm-m-m?" Katherine was having trouble keeping her mind clear. How could Janet be so calm at a time like this? "I . . . uh . . . I . . . Oh, yes, I called about the cabin we saw a few days ago. But, really, it can wait. Is there anything, anything at all, I can do for you?"

The two women talked a few more minutes and then Andy returned. Katherine rang off with visions of the two of them, bundled up, Janet leaning on Andy's shoulder for comfort and support, whispering gleefully, sharing things, helping each other through the day.

Tears, huge and hot, brimmed in Katherine's eyes. It was all too beautiful and, at the same time, too depressing to bear.

Katherine put the notepaper with the name and telephone number of the hospital Janet would be going to in a prominent spot on the desk. The paper from the day before—the list of messages she'd picked up after returning from Rimforest—demanded her attention and Katherine began returning calls.

The most intriguing of the lot was the one call she could not return until later on in the evening. Melanie James would be on the set of *Bright Promise* until at least six o'clock. She was surprised to have received a call from Melanie at all. Beyond a few noncommittal early-morning conversations, Katherine and Melanie had had little to do with each other. Theirs was a case of opposites *not* attracting. While Katherine was reserved and serious in her manner, Melanie was so bubbly and effervescent that Katherine had been tempted more than once to stuff a cork in the girl's mouth. And while it was perfectly natural for a new cast member to be slightly overanxious and energetic, there was something else about Melanie—a sureness, an edge of confidence in all her eagerness to please—that rang false and grated on Katherine's nerves.

The soft, purring sound of the intercom beside the front door interrupted Katherine's thoughts. The security guard at the lobby desk informed her that Larry Michaels was asking to come up.

As usual, he came through the door in a burst of effusive smiles and chatter, followed by the tinny jangle of gold chains and a cloud of billowing cigarette smoke.

"You ought to change services, kiddo," Larry muttered as he looked around for an ashtray, finally settling on a small Royal Worcester dish Katherine used to hold the keys to various cabinets and drawers. He unceremoniously dumped its contents and flicked ashes onto its bone-china surface. "I tried calling you all last night but it was like trying to get into Grandma's corset. They wouldn't ring me through. What's this?" His darting pale blue eyes fell on the paper atop the desk. "Melanie James? That little twit called my office three times, babbling about some housewarming that just wouldn't be the same without me. I had to listen to twenty minutes of what a great view she's got and a lot of crap about window seats and kidney-shaped pools."

"Her option must have been picked up ..." Katherine took an ashtray from an end-table drawer and rather pointedly made the switch, retrieving the delicate dish from Larry's hands before continuing, "... if she can afford to buy a house."

"Either that," Larry countered smugly, "or she's the latest member of a harem your producer's long-suffering wife pretends doesn't exist." He flopped down on the sofa and stretched out, his stacked heels rattling the glass of the coffee table. "My God, Katherine, you are *so* insulated! What is it with you? Are you naive or do you just not give a damn?"

"I'll take choice number two," Katherine answered dryly. "Melanie James's private life doesn't concern me."

"Well, it should, kiddo." Larry's eyes narrowed. "It sure as hell worries me. Hasn't it occurred to you how closely her character resembles a younger version of Leanne Cameron? Can't you feel her climbing up your back?"

Katherine was too stunned to reply. No, she hadn't given any serious thought to the similarity in the two characters. And now she waited, expecting a cold rush and a staggering fist of dread to slam into her gut.

Nothing. The expected reactions eluded her. Instead, Katherine felt curiosity, interest, even a detached calm.

"Luckily"—Larry grinned slyly—"the network doesn't, as yet, share your producer's confidence in Melanie's . . . um . . . talents. And that, my dear, is why I have ventured out in the midst of a smog alert and," he said, reaching into the inside pocket of his jacket with a flourish, "brought these papers for you to sign."

Now Katherine felt her stomach flutter and knot. She stared blindly at the folded papers and unthinkingly began to inch away.

"It's all here, Katherine." Larry waved the contracts over his head, oblivious of her response.

"Well, almost all. Three years, the same pay scale you were offered before, and twelve weeks no-commit every year."

"No-commit?" Katherine echoed dully, trying desperately to hold back the rise of panic in her voice.

"Yeah, those network lawyers are sneaky bastards! I had it worded that way so they couldn't come back later and try to schedule promos during the time you take off from the show."

"I see," Katherine stammered helplessly, joylessly. After a few moments she realized her fists were clenched tightly at her sides. She took a deep, shuddering breath and went to sit beside Larry. "I'd like to look the contracts over, Larry. Why don't you leave them with me over the weekend and I'll give you my decision on Monday?"

"Your decision?" Larry yelped on his way up off the sofa. "What do you mean 'your decision'? What's to decide here? Isn't this everything you demanded not less than four days ago?" He stood over her, glowering, his slight body trembling with indignation. "Goddammit, Katherine! What the hell do you want? I swear to you, this is the best we're going to do. There isn't any more. I—"

Katherine's brow creased with concern as she reached out and grabbed her agent's flailing hand. "I know that, Larry. Please calm down. It's a wonderful contract and you handled it all beautifully, but—"

"But?" Larry gasped and sagged back onto the

sofa again. "But what? What could possibly prevent you from signing this contract in blood if you had to? Katherine, it's a terrific deal!"

"I know it is," Katherine assured him gently, "but I need a little more time to . . ." She looked into Larry's astonished face and faltered. ". . . to think about—oh, this is so difficult to explain—to decide if I really *want* it anymore."

Another fifteen minutes passed before Katherine was able to put a halt to Larry's protestations and disbelief. Finally, with the promise that she would get in touch first thing Monday morning, he departed. Katherine put the contracts in the top drawer of the desk and promptly shoved the thought of them from her mind, instead focusing her attention on the calls she'd returned earlier. Without really thinking about it, she took out her month-at-a-glance calendar and began jotting down the appointments and obligations the calls had reminded her to note: a fitting Tuesday at the dressmaker's, a Wednesday-night session with the studio's publicity department, a charity dinner on Thursday night.

Seven days. The thought wiggled its way into her mind between the pauses of her pencil on the white paper of the calendar. Seven more days and she would be free to make the drive back to Rimforest and Joe. Seven more days and she would be sitting beside him, laughing, touching, a little arguing, a lot of making up.

On impulse, Katherine smiled and wrote the words "Baby Shea" across the top of the squares on the calendar. Janet's and Andy's baby would be home with them by the time Katherine got back to Rimforest. Suddenly that seemed more important than having her hair cut and styled for the photo session or taking the blue silk to the cleaner's so it would be out in time for the dinner.

Katherine was humming easily as she walked down the hall to her bedroom and got herself ready for an all-out assault on Beverly Hills' ritziest baby shops.

After a tiring day, the conversation Katherine had had with her answering service did little to improve her mood. Upon returning from her shopping spree, she had rung for her messages and was told that, among others, several calls had come in from a Dr. Mercer, most of them placed at the time Katherine was still at home. Katherine shakily explained that any calls from Joe were to be put through immediately. Upon returning his call, she found he'd left the same instructions with his service, but the insistent ringing in his bachelor apartment went on and on without answer. After several tries she gave up and started getting ready for the housewarming at Melanie James's home in the hills above Enicno. She dressed carefully, choosing an ice-blue cashmere sheath that she belted at the waist with a narrow black suede cincher. Her shoes boasted thin, spiky heels almost five inches high and slender straps of light blue and black that crisscrossed over her toes and fastened around her slim ankles.

Standing in front of the mirror in her bedroom, Katherine adjusted the clasp on a single-strand choker of tiny black onyx beads, admiring the overall effect of chic simplicity and struggling against the impulse to shed her elegant attire and forgo the evening's festivities.

The invitation was for nine o'clock. Katherine arrived fashionably late, thankful that Melanie had had the foresight to hire a valet parking service for evening. Cars lined the curbs up and down the three streets surrounding Melanie's new house. That, added to the idling cars behind Katherine as she got out of the Mercedes and handed her keys to the attendant, told her Melanie James had invited more than half the television community to her bash.

Katherine turned her coat over at the door and stepped into a teeming surge of bodies, rock music, mixed drinks, and a noise level just slightly less than deafening. Someone yelled her name and grabbed her arm from behind, dragging her off toward a corner. Joanne Talbot, a middle-aged actress who played the reliable mother figure on *Bright Promise*, was an eighteen-year veteran of the show. Joanne was already on her way to an early and sloppy departure from the party.

"Where *have* you been, Katherine?" The drink in Joanne's hand tipped dangerously close to Katherine's dress. "We've all been so concerned about this thing with the network. You *are* working it out, aren't you?"

Katherine nodded, smiling weakly, eager to extricate herself from the older woman's inquisitive, wheedling grasp.

"You look *gorgeous*, Katherine!" Another, deeper voice sounded close to her ear and she felt herself being pulled in an opposite direction.

"Hi, Riley." Katherine offered her cheek for an obligatory kiss from the actor who played the part of Leanne Cameron's latest conquest.

"You're a smart girl, Katherine, holding up the network brass the way you're doing." Riley beamed approvingly but there was something nervous in his eyes, a fear and desperation that glistened moistly on his face.

It hadn't occurred to Katherine before, but her decision was likely to affect other performers on the show. Riley Douglas' character had been introduced solely for the purpose of falling into Leanne's clutches. Was he strong enough, popular enough with the viewers, to endure on his own merit?

Katherine suddenly felt claustrophobic as a tiny current of guilt began to course through her body. She was about to excuse herself when Riley launched into a lengthy monologue about the made-for-TV movie he'd just tested for.

"The role isn't large," his voice droned on, "but pivotal and, for myself, I'd rather have an important secondary part than a weak lead. This character has inner . . ."

Katherine's eyes began to lose focus. Why had she come, when she knew how much she would hate it? These functions were always the same. The topic of conversation never changed: I and me, the two most important people in the universe. More deals were made at these showcase parties than in the offices of the networks. Everyone was "on" from the moment he walked through the door.

A bright flash popped in Katherine's face, leaving her with dancing white spots before her eyes. Her mouth tightened as she cursed Melanie for not leaving anything to chance. The girl had hired a crew of photographers to shoot a pictorial record of the party, ostensibly to provide her guests with a memento. It was an old and very tired publicity trick. Heaven help the wrong people caught together at the wrong moment. Their photo was certain to end up on the inside pages of a gossip publication with a caption reading "So and So at newcomer Melanie James's gala housewarming." Melanie would have her name in print and the people involved would be painfully reminded that discretion was their only protection in the future.

Riley Douglas was winding down his soliloquy, his eyes already darting about for another likely victim. Katherine breathed a sigh of relief when he moved like quicksilver to latch on to the arm of the show's assistant producer, a harmless, ineffectual man who had made a career of patiently listening to and promptly forgetting the actors' seemingly endless lists of woes.

Looking around, Katherine realized there was not one person at the party she truly wished to seek out and spend some time with. Not even one. She was sick to death of talking and dancing with men who were more concerned about their looks than she was with her own. She was tired of women who were brittle and afraid, of conversations that never seemed to advance beyond movie deals, auditions, and callbacks.

As she made her way outside, Katherine was jostled, hugged, and kissed by almost everyone she passed. Good to see you, Katherine. Glad to have you back, darling. Where *have* you been?

It was a crisp night, one of those California nights that made her wonder where people got the idea that L.A. enjoyed year-round eighty-degree weather.

The sound of piped-in rock music faded behind her as Katherine made her way to the pool area. There were a few people milling around, but no one Katherine knew. She passed without comment and went to sit in a poolside chair.

Looking up, Katherine could see the long expanse of floor-to-ceiling glass that ran across the entire back of the house. Inside, the party was going full swing. Every now and then the sliding door opened and a blast of music and laughter briefly filtered down to her.

Katherine smiled slightly. She could see Melanie, surrounded by a group made up almost entirely of males, her head thrown back, hands waving about to settle first on one man and then another.

She's really enjoying herself, Katherine mused without rancor. At least she acts as though she's having the time of her life.

Melanie appeared to be completely relaxed, as though she thrived on the attention and high degree of pressure of her chosen profession. She enjoyed seeking out the "big break" like a cat sniffing out a saucer of milk.

Good luck, Katherine thought, mentally saluting the girl's efforts. And may you never find yourself sitting at the fringes, wondering if the place you've arrived at is the place you wanted when you started out.

Chapter Ten

❧

Saturday morning found Katherine lying fully dressed on her bed, flat on her back, staring at the ceiling. She had been that way for hours. A mimeographed, typewritten proposal of the story line for the next three months of *Bright Promise* dropped off by Larry Michaels while Katherine was at Melanie's party, lay discarded at her side. An added sheet took the character of Leanne Cameron on for an additional three months. Larry was obviously trying to nudge Katherine in the right direction by letting her know the writers' plans for Leanne's upcoming escapades: husband stealing, two affairs, an abortion (Leanne's third), and (surprise!) attempted murder. All in all, it was a charming little scenario, your ordinary, everyday, true-to-life scheming and plotting.

Katherine had awakened at seven, fixed herself a pot of coffee, showered, dressed, and stretched out to read the plot line Larry had left with the security guard. At eight o'clock she'd set it aside and seriously begun to question her actions and responses of the last two days.

Okay, she had to admit, she was *looking* for reasons to find fault in everything she'd seen and done since leaving Rimforest. It wasn't the people or the smog or the pressures. The acting community was like a small, isolated microcosm of people anywhere—some good, some bad, self-involved and selfless. She would find those differences wherever she went. At Melanie's party Katherine had made a point of singling out the worst examples in her circle of acquaintances, completely ignoring the patient merits of Michael Koss, *Bright Promise*'s director, or the sweet enthusiasm of Angela Laird, the show's reigning ingenue. Both of them had been in attendance, but Katherine had shunned more than a passing greeting because she chose *not* to be reminded. It was easier that way. She could cringe and tell herself: That's a good reason for getting out. These grasping, conniving people will bury me.

But the truth was, only Katherine could bury Katherine. She had survived nearly fifteen years, and, for reasons she could not even begin to understand, the viewing public had clasped her to their collective heart. If she really wanted it, she was strong enough to survive another fifteen years.

No, it wasn't the people. And it wasn't even the quality of her life. Katherine lived in an electronically guarded fortress, ten stories above the street, not because she was endangered by the elements but because she was a solitary, private person and the isolation had, at one time, applealed to her. It no longer served that purpose. It was as simple as that.

So, if it wasn't the people or her physical surroundings that made her so desperately unhappy, what was it? Pressure? Professional demands? No, she knew she responded well under pressure. And if she were going to be perfectly honest with herself, she knew she could never sit around watching sunsets all the time. She had been busy all her life with one thing or another and would probably always be a compulsive worker.

It was all so simple, so clear when she got past the trivialities. Katherine was in love, and that love was the single most important aspect of her exsistence. She couldn't define or measure it in terms of who had to give up what in order to make it work. Was loving and living together ever truly a fifty-fifty proposition?

Katherine's gaze wandered to the suitcases she'd packed and set beside her bedroom door. Taking a deep breath, she grinned and reached for the telephone.

"Larry? Sorry to call so early, but I'm just on my way out the door and I wanted to—"

"You got the script line, right?" Larry's sleepy voice brightened considerably. "I knew you'd like it. Leanne's going to be a pretty busy lady, huh?"

"No, Larry, she isn't." There was no easy way of saying it, so Katherine just barreled on. "I'm not going to sign the contracts, Larry. I'm leaving now, for Rimforest."

"No you're not!" Larry's voice shrilled through the phone line. "Stay right where you are! I'll be over in a half-hour. We can talk about this. You—"

"I'm leaving," Katherine repeated. "Don't come over. I won't be here." She softened her voice, imagining the stunned expression on Larry's face. "The studio will just have to arrange a neat little

death for Leanne while she's off in New York.
Like you said, Larry, it's done all the time."

"It's that hick doctor, isn't it?" Larry's tone
implied a personal betrayal. His short, cynical
laugh taunted Katherine. "Well, you'll be back in
a month, kiddo, I promise you. Nobody ever stays
away. You'll go crazy in the boondocks with nothing to do but watch the snow fall."

"I'll go crazy if I *don't* go!" Katherine knew
there was no point in trying to justify anything
as elusive as love to Larry, but she said it anyway.
"I'm not giving up anything, Larry. I'm changing.
And it's a good change, at least for me. It might
take some getting used to, but I'm going to love
having the freedom and time to do just that! I've
finally realized I can't blame anyone else for the
quality of my life up until now, but I *can* do
something positive to turn it around. I love someone and he loves me. Nothing is more important
than that."

"Don't do this, Katherine." Larry's voice had
an edge of panic to it. "I've seen it happen a
hundred times. You'll want to come back but
there won't be anything here for you."

"I won't come back," Katherine assured him,
her conviction ringing clear in her own ears.
"Everything I want is in another place. Be happy
for me, Larry. I have to go now, but I'll call you
sometime next week to see how things are going.
By the way," she added, hoping the new revenue
would someday compensate for the financial loss
Larry would suffer at her instigation, "do you
remember when Melanie James asked you to rep-
resent her? Well, I'd take her up on it, if I were

you. The kid's ..." Katherine laughed again at her own usage of one of Larry's favorite phrases. "The kid's a real comer."

The return drive took longer than Katherine expected, stretching from two to three hours and then four. Again, she'd caught the weekend traffic to Big Bear's ski lifts, and more than once she was seriously tempted to roll down the car window and shout, "Don't you people have anything better to do than clutter up the roads when I'm on my way to changing the course of my life?"

Prudently Katherine decided against such a drastic display of impatience and, instead, made a solemn promise to herself. She would never, never leave the quiet and serenity of their home on a winter weekend. Shopping, visiting, skiing, anything having the remotest connection with highway travel would be accomplished midweek.

When at last Katherine made the turn to Rimforest, she drove straight to Joe's office and swung around back through the alley to the apartment entrance. The Blazer was nowhere in sight. Still, she pulled into the stall and parked.

Now what? He could be anywhere on the mountain—or in San Bernadino, for that matter. Katherine sighed in disappointment and tried to narrow the options as clearheadedly as she could.

It was Saturday afternoon. Janet had been delivered of a healthy nine-pound baby boy at the ungodly hour of four in the morning. By all rights, Joe should have been inside sleeping. Short of an emergency, there was no reason to believe he was either at the hospital or out making a house call.

Katherine squinted toward the door. Didn't small-town doctors leave chalkboard messages beside the door? Messages that read "Delivering Shea baby, back at sundown" or "Gone fishing" or some such tidbit of information? Katherine had seen it in a movie, and right now it seemed like a pretty good idea.

She grinned at the preposterous notion and got back to the serious business of tracking Joe down. She immediately dismissed the thought that he might, at that very moment, be on his way into L.A. Wild horses couldn't drag him off the mountain, especially after the way she'd run out on him again. He was too stubborn and bullheaded for that. And yet, he *had* tried to phone her.

Oh, God, Katherine groaned helplessly, I could go on like this all day long. Wondering and guessing. Why isn't he home?

Home! Suddenly Katherine knew exactly where to find him. She slammed the car into reverse and headed back down the alley and onto the southbound highway leading to Lake Gregory. She had a terrible sense of direction but she zeroed in on the nearly completed house on Montreaux Drive with the instincts of a homing pigeon.

And there it was, parked on the newly paved concrete drive: Joe's Blazer.

Katherine pulled up behind the Blazer and turned off the ignition, pausing a moment to check her reflection in the rearview mirror. Her appearance would have no real bearing on whether or not he was glad to see her back in his life again, but every little bit helped.

The dark brown crewneck sweater, worn over a forest-green shirt, matched her eyes. Hours of sitting in the car had stretched out her tan corduroys, but they were so tight to begin with that the shape wasn't a total loss.

Just a dab of fresh lipstick—why was her hand trembling?—and Katherine got out of the car and started for the door. It was ajar, and something, a fluttering sensation in her throat, stopped her cold before she took the last few steps that would bring her face to face with Joe.

What if he wasn't happy to see her? Had she run out on him one time too many? And would he believe her when she said she was back to stay?

Katherine was still rooted to the spot as she heard the thud of leather soles advancing toward her. The sound got louder, closer, and with each step Katherine's eyes grew wider and more uncertain.

Joe passed by directly in front of her, not more than four feet away, his handsome face a study of preoccupied concentration, an intense focus that wavered and dissolved as he spun back in her direction.

"Katie!" Confusion, disbelief, surprise, and, finally, delight registered across his face in the fleeting of a few split seconds. Then Joe's face broke into a warm grin. "Why are you lurking in the doorway?" He set down the heavy toolbox he held and reached her in two powerful strides, his arms slipping around her waist, his lips lightly brushing the corner of her mouth.

"May I come in?" Foolish tears swelled in her throat and threatened to spill out over her cheeks. Katherine swallowed hard and attempted a smile that trembled expectantly on her lips.

In answer, Joe gently guided her from the foyer into the kitchen, where he'd been working only minutes before. There was as yet no furniture in the house, so he put both hands at Katherine's waist and lifted her onto the counter. She sat there a moment, legs dangling over the side, while Joe got a paper cup and filled it with water from the faucet, using the time to look around at what he'd been doing all day.

The last of the cabinet and drawer hardware was in place. Wallpaper swatches—everything from colonial copper prints to scrolled recipes bordered by ivy vines—lay scattered all over the tiled floor. Middle-of-the-road rock music played softly from a transistor radio sitting atop an almond-colored dishwasher that had yet to be installed.

When Joe came back with the cup of water, he put it in Katherine's hands and watched her down it in two swallows.

"You're early," he stated flatly, carefully, as he stood slightly back. "I didn't expect to see you until next weekend."

"I canceled all my other appointments." Katherine forced a saucy, bantering tone. "I decided I needed indefinite treatment by my doctor."

It wasn't working. She was behaving in a casual, offhand manner when what she really wanted to do was throw herself into Joe's embrace and tell him . . . Katherine felt the tears rise again. How much time would it take before she got out of the habit of "playing" her emotions instead of living them?

She took a deep breath and started again. "I've quit the show." She shrugged gracefully. "It wasn't nearly as traumatic as I thought it would be. Actually, it was pretty easy. I love you, Joey. I want you more than I want anything else, so . . ." Katherine looked into his eyes and sighed happily, feeling warm and safe in the glow of love she saw reflected there. "Here I am again. I don't know if anything between us will ever be easy, but it's sure never going to be dull."

Katherine lifted her legs straight out in front of her, crossed her ankles around Joe's back, and lifted her arms to encircle his neck. "Well, say something, would you?" she murmured against his lips, her eyes fluttering at the feel of his hard, hungry body responding to her touch. "Do you still want me?"

"Yes," Joe drawled slowly, drawing his answer out until it felt like a caress. "I want you." His mouth closed over hers, stealing away Katherine's breath with its deep, tantalizing passion. Joe's fingers moved gently over her cheeks, lifting her face to his as he slowly pulled away. "I need you," he whispered, and then impishly grinned, "to help me decide on the wallpaper and carpet we're going to put in this place. Except for my taste in women," he said as he lifted her off the counter and set her on her feet, "I've got a lousy sense of style."

Katherine broke into a contented laugh. His timing left a lot to be desired, but they had all the time they needed to work on that and anything else that came up.

"Where are you going?" she asked, putting her hand on his arm as he moved off toward the kitchen door.

"First things first! My lesson in interior design can wait. Right now I'm going out to the truck." Joe's blue eyes sparkled with a gleam that tugged at Katherine's heart. "I'm going to drive down to the village for a bottle of wine." He returned to Katherine and encircled her tightly in his arms. "And then I'm coming back and I'm going to take the sleeping bags out of the back of the truck."

A strand of golden-brown hair fell softly over his brow as he bent to whisper, "I'm going to spread the bags out in the living room and uncork the wine. And *then*"—Joe's voice was heavy and warm against Katherine's lips—"we're going to light a fire."

TELL US YOUR OPINIONS AND RECEIVE A FREE COPY
OF THE RAPTURE NEWSLETTER.

Thank you for filling out our questionnaire. Your response to the following questions will help us to bring you more and better books. In appreciation of your help we will send you a free copy of the Rapture Newsletter.

1. Book Title:_____

   Book #:_____ (5-7)

2. Using the scale below how would you rate this book on the following features? Please write in one rating from 0–10 for each feature in the spaces provided. Ignore bracketed numbers.

(Poor) 0 1 2 3 4 5 6 7 8 9 10 (Excellent)
                                            0–10 Rating

Overall Opinion of Book. . . . . _____ (8)
Plot/Story. . . . . _____ (9)
Setting/Location. _____ (10)
Writing Style. . . . . _____ (11)
Dialogue. . . . . _____ (12)
Love Scenes. . . . . _____ (13)
Character Development:
Heroine:. . . . . _____ (14)
Hero:. . . . . _____ (15)
Romantic Scene on Front Cover. . . . . _____ (16)
Back Cover Story Outline . . . . _____ (17)
First Page Excerpts. . . . . _____ (18)

3. What is your: Education: Age:_____ (20-22)

      High School ( )1   4 Yrs. College ( )3
      2 Yrs. College ( )2   Post Grad   ( )4 (23)

4. Print Name:_____

   Address:_____

   City:_____State:_____Zip:_____

   Phone # (   )_____ (25)

Thank you for your time and effort. Please send to New American Library, Rapture Romance Research Department, 1633 Broadway, New York, NY 10019.

RAPTURE ROMANCE

*Provocative and sensual,
passionate and tender—
the magic and mystery of love
in all its many guises*

Coming next month

SEPTEMBER SONG by Lisa Moore. Swearing her career came first, Lauren Rose faced the challenge of her life in Mark Landrill's arms, for she had to choose between the work she thrived on—and a passion that left her both fulfilled and enslaved . . .

A MOUNTAIN MAN by Megan Ashe. For Kelly March, Josh Munroe's beloved mountain world was a haven where she could prove her independence, but Josh—who tormented her with desire—resented the intrusion. Could Kelly prove she was worth his love—and, if she did, would she lose all she'd fought to achieve?

THE KNAVE OF HEARTS by Estelle Edwards. Brilliant young lawyer Kate Sewell had no defense against carefree riverboat gambler Hal Lewis. But could Kate risk her career—even for the ecstasy his love promised?

BEYOND ALL STARS by Melinda McKenzie. For astronaut Ann Lafton, working with Commander Ed Saber brought emotional chaos that jeopardized their NASA shuttle mission. But Ann couldn't stop dreaming that this sensuous lover would fly her to the stars . . .

DREAMLOVER by JoAnn Robb. Painter K.L. Michaels needed Hunter St. James to pull off a daring masquerade, but she didn't count on losing her relaxed lifestyle as their wild love affair unfolded. Could their nights of sensual fireworks make up for their daily battles?

A LOVE SO FRESH by Marilyn Davids. Loving Ben Heron was everything Anna Markham needed. But she considered marriage a trap, and Ben, too, had been burned before. Passion drew them together, but was their rapture enough to overcome the obstacles they faced?

RAPTURE ROMANCE

Provocative and sensual, passionate and tender— the magic and mystery of love in all its many guises

New Titles Available Now

To order, use coupon on the next page.

RAPTURE ROMANCE

Provocative and sensual,
passionate and tender—
the magic and mystery of love
in all its many guises

Buy them at your local

bookstore or use coupon

on next page for ordering.

RAPTURE ROMANCE

Provocative and sensual, passionate and tender— the magic and mystery of love in all its many guises

SPECIAL $1.00 REBATE OFFER
WHEN YOU BUY
FOUR RAPTURE ROMANCES

To receive your cash refund, send:

1. This coupon: To qualify for the $1.00 refund, this coupon, completed with your name and address, must be used. (Certificate may not be reproduced)

2. Proof of purchase: Print, on the reverse side of this coupon, the *title* of the books, the *numbers* of the books (on the upper right hand of the front cover preceding the price), and the U.P.C. numbers (on the back covers) on your next four purchases.

3. Cash register receipts, with prices circled to:
   Rapture Romance $1.00 Refund Offer
   P.O. Box NB037
   El Paso, Texas 79977

Offer good only in the U.S. and Canada. Limit one refund/response per household for any group of four Rapture Romance titles. Void where prohibited, taxed or restricted. Allow 6–8 weeks for delivery. Offer expires March 31, 1984.

NAME_____

ADDRESS_____

CITY_____STATE_____ZIP_____

SPECIAL $1.00 REBATE OFFER
WHEN YOU BUY
FOUR RAPTURE ROMANCES

See complete details on reverse

1. Book Title _____

Book Number 451-_____

U.P.C. Number 7116200195-_____

2. Book Title _____

Book Number 451-_____

U.P.C. Number 7116200195-_____

3. Book Title _____

Book Number 451-_____

U.P.C. Number 7116200195-_____

4. Book Title _____

Book Number 451-_____

U.P.C. Number 7116200195-_____

—— U.P.C. Number

```
0   |||||||||||||||||  18003  ||||||||
         SAMPLE
       7 11162 00195
```